2024

Training

mit Original-Prüfungen

Hauptschule Niedersachsen

Englisch 10. Klasse

STARK

Bildnachweis

Deckblätter: S. 1: © 123rf.com, S. 75: © wavebreakmedia. Shutterstock
S. 7: Taxis New York © Tono Balaguer. 123rf.com; Känguru © Christopher Meder. Shutterstock, Safari © luisapuccini.123rf.com, Kreditkarte © wavebreakmedia ltd. Shutterstock, Münzen © Oliver Hoffmann. Shutterstock, 5-Pfund-Schein © Can Stock Photo/aaronamat, Digitalziffern © DVARG. Shutterstock, Eis mit Kirsche © karen roach. Shutterstock, Fish and Chips © Janet Faye Hastings. Shutterstock; S. 8: Block Papier © peshkova. 123rf.com, Buchcover © foxie. Shutterstock, Farbtöpfe © Petrenko Andriy. Shutterstock, T-Shirt © Tarzhanova. Shutterstock, Pullover © indigolotos. Shutterstock, Filzstifte © Ruslan Kerimov. Shutterstock, Buntstifte © kamomeen. Shutterstock, schwarze Katze von der Seite (links und rechts) © Eric Isselee. Shutterstock, Katzen von hinten © Can Stock Photo/IvonneWierink; S. 9: © sergioboccardo. Shutterstock; S. 10: © Eric Isselée. Fotolia.com; S. 11: © Andrey Bayda. Shutterstock; S. 12: Fish and Chips in Tüte © francesco83. 123rf.com, Schild „Fish and Chips" © Michael Urmann. Shutterstock; S. 13: © stockbroker. 123rf.com; S. 14: © Fabien Monteil. Shutterstock; S. 18: Illustration Flugzeug © iimages. 123rf.com, Prozent-Würfel © FreshPaint. Shutterstock, Kochlöffel © arigato. Shutterstock, Silhouette jubelnde Menge © dwphotos. Shutterstock; S. 19: Frau mit Hanteln © mast3r. Shutterstock, ältere Dame mit Pflegerin © Alexander Raths. Shutterstock, Paar am Meer; © Alex Jackson. Shutterstock, Illustration Auto © kolopach. Shutterstock; S. 21: Lilly © Andresr. Shutterstock, Kathy © ostill. Shutterstock, Simon © 123rf.com, Jamal © Mikie Flippo. Shutterstock, Charlie © michaeljung. Shutterstock; S. 23: Eva © Rido. Shutterstock, Tom © Antonio Jorge Nunes. Shutterstock, Harry © kadettmann. 123rf.com, Kim © kurhan. 123rf.com, Amy © Kinga. Shutterstock; S. 24: public domain; S. 25: © FloridaStock. Shutterstock; S. 26: US Airways Flight 1549 in the Hudson River New York © CC BY-SA 2.0; S. 27: © Foto: Frederick J. Phillips/wikipedia, CC BY-SA 2.0; S. 28: © 724258. Shutterstock; S. 30: © Alisonh29/Dreamstime.com; S. 33: © daisydaisy. 123rf.com; S. 34: Schild „No Swimming" © 123rf. com, Illustration gesprungenes Eis © seamartini. 123rf.com, Schild „Smoke free" © Robert J. Beyers II. Shutterstock; S. 35: Illustration Löwenkopf © Ant_art. Shutterstock, Poster „Autumn Festival" © Vector Tradition SM. Fotolia.com; S. 37: Schild „Wi-fi area" © ARENA Creative. Shutterstock; S. 39: Tafel „Breakfast Menu" © Kevin George/Dreamstime.com; S. 41: Schild „Stay on trail"; © Candus Camera. Shutterstock, Schild „Attention" © Ricky Corey. 123rf.com; S. 42: Schild „Spielplatz" © Can Stock Photo/oliwkowygaj; S. 43: Hamburger Hafen © Can Stock Photo/CarmenSteiner; S. 51: Regenschirm © 123rf.com, Frau mit Gitarre © spaxiax. Shutterstock; S. 52: © LIGHTFIELD STUDIOS. Fotolia.com; S. 53: Mann in Smartphone vertieft © Maridav. Shutterstock, Fuß tritt auf Bananenschale © ESUN7756. Shutterstock, Illustration Fragezeichen © Georgios Kollidas. Shutterstock; S. 54: Bank in Park © Felix Mittermeier/pixabay, Kolosseum © abadesign. Shutterstock; S. 55: Schulmotive © 123rf.com; S. 56: Zug © 123rf.com; S. 57: griechische Insel © Kwiatek7. Shutterstock; S. 58: Maske und Rose © Scott Rothstein. Shutterstock; S. 59: Lion King-Aufführung © Can Stock Photo/tana; S. 60: Hotel © Can Stock Photo/styf22; S. 61: Rollkoffer mit Urlaubssymbolen; © abdurahman. 123rf.com, Bügeleisen © Neveshkin Nikolay. Shutterstock, gefaltetes Hemd © belchonock. 123rf.com; S. 62: Wahlurne © happymay. Shutterstock; S. 70: © Jan Martin Will/Dreamstime.com; S. 73: Mädchen vor Computer © Monkey Business Images Ltd/Dreamstime.com, Mädchen traurig © Dawn Shearer-Simonetti. Shutterstock

18. ergänzte Auflage
www.stark-verlag.de

Inhalt

Hinweise, Tipps und Übungsaufgaben zu den Kompetenzbereichen

Sobald die Original-Prüfungsaufgaben 2023 freigegeben sind, können sie als **PDF** auf der Plattform **MyStark** heruntergeladen werden (Zugangscode auf der Umschlaginnenseite vorne im Buch).

Hörtexte

Hinweis: Die Audio-Dateien kannst du ebenfalls über die Plattform MyStark abrufen.

Hörtexte Übungsaufgaben gesprochen von: Esther Gilvray, Nadine Groß, Daniel Holzberg, Jennifer Mikulla, Veronica Stivala, Benjamin Tendler, Roger Voight; Soundeffekte: pacdv, freesound

Trainingsteil und Lösungen verfasst von: Birte Bendrich („Speaking"), Heike Burfeind, Paul Jenkinson („Listening" und „Reading"), Redaktion
Lösungen Original-Prüfungsaufgaben: Birte Bendrich

Vorwort

Liebe Schülerin, lieber Schüler,

in diesem Buch findest du die Original-Prüfungsaufgaben 2020–2022 und (in digitaler Form) die Aufgaben 2023 sowie Übungen zu den Fertigkeitsbereichen der offiziellen Prüfung. Es eignet sich somit ideal zur selbstständigen und gezielten Vorbereitung auf die **Prüfung 2024**. Du kannst mit diesem Buch aber auch schon **ab der 9. Klasse** dein Englisch **gezielt** verbessern und dich auf **Klassenarbeiten** optimal vorbereiten.

- Die **Übungsaufgaben** widmen sich den Kompetenzbereichen *Listening*, *Reading*, *Mediating*, *Writing* und *Speaking*. In den ersten Abschnitten erfährst du jeweils, welche Anforderungen auf dich zukommen können und wie du dich am besten darauf vorbereitest. Anhand der Übungen kannst du trainieren, wie man mit möglichen Aufgabenstellungen umgeht und sie erfolgreich löst.
- Im Kapitel *Writing* findest du u. a. **hilfreiche Wendungen**, die dir in den unterschiedlichen Bereichen nützlich sein werden und dir das selbstständige Verfassen von Texten erleichtern. Mithilfe der Tipps und Aufgaben im Kapitel *Speaking* kannst du dich auch auf die mündliche Prüfung („oral exam“) vorbereiten.
- Die Bereiche **Wortschatz** und **Grammatik** werden zwar nicht gesondert abgeprüft, aber sie sind wichtig für die Bearbeitung der Aufgaben in den anderen Kompetenzbereichen. Deshalb stellen wir dir auf der Plattform **MyStark** eine **digitale Kurzgrammatik** zur Verfügung, in der alle wichtigen grammatischen Themen knapp erläutert und an Beispielsätzen veranschaulicht werden. Zudem gibt es in einem Video Tipps zum Vokabellernen. Anhand von **interaktiven Aufgaben** zu Wortschatz und Grammatik kannst du deine Kenntnisse auch gleich testen.
- Mithilfe der **Original-Prüfungsaufgaben** der letzten Jahre kannst du eine Abschlussprüfung vollständig durcharbeiten und deine Kenntnisse unter Prüfungsbedingungen testen. Die Original-Prüfungsaufgaben 2023 stehen, sobald zur Veröffentlichung freigegeben, auf der Plattform **MyStark**.
- Das beiliegende **Lösungsheft** enthält alle Lösungen und ausführliche Lösungsvorschläge mit praktischen Tipps und Hinweisen zum Bearbeiten der Aufgaben.

Sollten nach Erscheinen dieses Bandes noch wichtige Änderungen in der Abschlussprüfung vom Kultusministerium bekannt gegeben werden, findest du aktuelle Informationen dazu ebenfalls auf der Plattform **MyStark**.

Viel Spaß beim Üben und viel Erfolg in der Prüfung!

Hinweise zu den digitalen Zusätzen

Auf die folgenden digitalen Inhalte zu deinem Band kannst du online über die Plattform **MyStark** zugreifen. Verwende dazu deinen persönlichen **Zugangscode** auf der Umschlaginnenseite vorne im Buch.

PDF der Original-Prüfungsaufgaben mit Lösungen 2023

Um dir die Prüfung 2023 so schnell wie möglich zur Verfügung zu stellen, sind die Aufgaben und Lösungen zur Prüfung nicht im Buch abgedruckt, sondern erscheinen in digitaler Form.

Hördateien

Die Plattform **MyStark** enthält auch die MP3-Dateien zu den Hörverstehenstexten der Übungsaufgaben und der Original-Prüfungsaufgaben.

Kurzgrammatik

In der Kurzgrammatik werden alle wichtigen grammatischen Themen knapp erläutert und an Beispielsätzen veranschaulicht.

Web-App „MindCards"

Die Web-App „MindCards" ermöglicht es dir, am Smartphone **hilfreiche Wendungen** zu den Kompetenzen „Writing" und „Speaking" zu wiederholen. Über nebenstehende QR-Codes oder die unten angegebenen Links gelangst du zu den MindCards.
https://www.stark-verlag.de/mindcards/writing-1
https://www.stark-verlag.de/mindcards/speaking-1

Writing

Speaking

Interaktives Training

Zusätzlich zu den Aufgaben im Buch hast du die Möglichkeit, **Grundlagen** wie **Wortschatz und Grammatik** interaktiv zu üben. Diese Grundlagen brauchst du u. a. auch für die Kompetenzbereiche **Hör- und Leseverstehen**, die du ebenfalls digital am PC oder Laptop trainieren kannst:

- „Listening Comprehension" – unterschiedliche Hörtexte (*Announcements*, *Conversations* und Dialoge) mit Aufgaben zum Hörverstehen
- „Reading Comprehension" – Sachtexte mit verschiedenen Aufgabenformaten zum Leseverstehen
- „Vocabulary Practice" – Aufgaben z. B. zu Wortfeldern, Definitionen, *Opposites* und *Words in context*
- „Grammar Practice" – Aufgaben zu einzelnen grammatischen Strukturen (inkl. Lernvideos)

Hinweise zur Abschlussprüfung

Schülerinnen und Schüler der 10. Klassen an Schulformen, die nach den Kerncurricula der Hauptschule unterrichtet werden, nehmen an den zentralen Prüfungen zum Erwerb des **Sekundarabschlusses I – Hauptschulabschluss/ Realschulabschluss oder des Erweiterten Sekundarabschlusses I** teil. Die Prüfungsaufgaben werden auf der Grundlage der Kerncurricula der Hauptschule/Oberschule und der Bildungsstandards erstellt.

Bearbeitungsdauer

Die Bearbeitungszeiten für die schriftlichen Prüfungen wurden vom Kultusministerium folgendermaßen festgelegt:

Deutsch	180 Minuten
Mathematik	150 Minuten
Englisch	120 Minuten

Die schriftliche Prüfung besteht aus mehreren Teilen. In der Abschlussprüfung 2020 wurde neben den Bereichen *Listening*, *Reading* und *Writing* auch der Bereich *Mediating* geprüft. In den Jahren 2021 bis 2023 ist die Sprachmittlung in den Abschlussprüfungen pandemiebedingt entfallen. Erkundige dich vorab bei deiner Lehrkraft, ob *Mediating* 2024 wieder Teil der Abschlussprüfung sein wird oder nicht.

Ablauf der schriftlichen Prüfung

- In der Prüfung hast du zunächst 15 Minuten Zeit, beide Aufgabensets zum Kompetenzbereich *Writing* zu sichten und dich für ein Aufgabenset zu entscheiden. Das nicht gewählte Set wird wieder abgegeben. Erst jetzt beginnt der eigentliche Prüfungszeitraum.
- Für den sich anschließenden Prüfungsteil *Listening* stehen dir ca. 30 Minuten zur Verfügung. Die Länge dieses Prüfungsteils hängt von der Spiellänge der verwendeten Audioquelle ab.
- Für die restlichen Teile stehen dann ca. 90 Minuten zur Verfügung. Dabei solltest du für den Prüfungsteil *Writing* die längste Bearbeitungsdauer einplanen.
- Die Hauptschulabschlussprüfung ist in Aufgaben für den **E-Kurs** und den **G-Kurs** unterteilt, die an das jeweilige Niveau (Niveau A2+ und A2) des Kurses angepasst sind.

Hinweise, Tipps und Übungsaufgaben zu den Kompetenzbereichen

1 Kompetenzbereich: Listening

Zu verstehen, was andere Menschen in der Fremdsprache sagen, ist eine wichtige sprachliche Fertigkeit im alltäglichen Leben. Wenn du in einem englischsprachigen Land bist, sprichst du viel mehr mit anderen Menschen, als dass du ihnen etwas schreibst. Es hilft dir also sehr, dich in einem anderen Land zurechtzufinden, wenn du z. B. eine Wegbeschreibung verstehst. Deshalb ist es wichtig, das Hörverstehen intensiv zu üben. Die Texte der Höraufgaben in diesem Buch und in der Abschlussprüfung spiegeln daher auch Sprech- und Hörsituationen wider, die einem im Alltag begegnen können, z. B. ein Interview im Radio, ein Podcast, oder ein Gespräch zwischen zwei oder mehr Personen.

1.1 Strategien zum Kompetenzbereich „Listening“

Ablauf des Hörverstehensteils in der Abschlussprüfung

Hier ist es ganz wichtig, dass du selbst einmal die Höraufgaben der letzten zentralen Abschlussprüfung ausprobierst. Der Hörverstehenstest läuft folgendermaßen ab:

- Die Anweisungen und Texte werden euch vorgespielt. Die Texte hört ihr dabei immer zweimal.
- Dir wird zuerst Zeit gegeben, dich mit den Arbeitsanweisungen und Aufgaben vertraut zu machen.
- Nun geht der Hörverstehenstest los. Wenn ein Hörtext das erste Mal vorgespielt wird, kannst du die Aufgaben bereits bearbeiten.
- Wenn der Hörtext wiederholt wird, kannst du deine Antworten überprüfen oder noch vervollständigen.
- Zum Schluss wird dir noch einmal Zeit gegeben, alles durchzusehen.

TIPP

Vor dem ersten Hören

- Lies dir die Aufgaben genau durch. Achte dabei auf Schlüsselwörter, die auf die richtige Antwort hinweisen.
- Höre genau auf die Anweisungen.

Beim ersten Hören

- Höre genau zu. Worum geht es im Text? Achte dabei wieder auf Schlüsselwörter.
- Verwende beim ersten Hören evtl. einen Bleistift, damit du noch etwas ändern kannst.

Beim zweiten Hören

- Die Fragen folgen der Reihenfolge im Text. Wenn du eine Frage beim ersten Hören nicht beantworten konntest, dann versuche, beim zweiten Hören die Stelle im Text zu finden.
- Bearbeite möglichst alle Aufgaben. Auch wenn du die richtige Lösung nicht weißt, kreuze z. B. bei *Multiple Choice*-Aufgaben eine Antwort an. Vielleicht liegst du ja richtig.
- Überprüfe noch einmal deine Antworten.

Vorgehen beim Üben

Bevor du dich an die Bearbeitung der Original-Abschlussprüfung wagst, die in diesem Buch enthalten ist, kannst du anhand der Übungsaufgaben schon einmal Schritt für Schritt für die Prüfung trainieren. Versuche, wie in der echten Prüfung, die Aufgaben nur durch Zuhören zu bearbeiten. Erst wenn du überhaupt nicht auf die richtige Lösung kommst, solltest du die Hörverstehenstexte im Lösungsteil lesen. Bei der Bearbeitung der Übungsaufgaben kannst du wie folgt vorgehen:

- Lies dir erst einmal, wie in der Prüfung, die Aufgaben durch. Hast du sie verstanden? Frage dich, ob du die Hörsituation schon erkennst – handelt es sich z. B. um ein Interview? Wichtig ist, dass du auf Schlüsselwörter achtest, die dir einen Hinweis auf die Lösung geben. Falls nötig, kannst du auch das Wörterbuch zu Hilfe nehmen. In der Prüfung solltest du es aufgrund des Zeitaufwands nur sparsam einsetzen.
- Höre dir den entsprechenden Text nun einmal an, sodass du weißt, worum es geht. Achte wiederum auf Schlüsselwörter (z. B. „o'clock" oder „am", wenn nach der Uhrzeit gefragt wird). Manchmal geben auch Hintergrundgeräusche einen Hinweis auf die Lösung.
- Höre dir den Text jetzt noch einmal an und versuche dabei, alle Aufgaben zu lösen. Wenn dir dies immer noch Probleme bereitet, kannst du den Text noch ein drittes oder viertes Mal anhören. Versuche dabei, nicht in die Lösungen zu schauen.
- Erst wenn du alles bearbeitet hast oder gar nicht weiterkommst, kannst du deine Antworten mit den Lösungen im Lösungsteil vergleichen.
- Während der Überprüfung solltest du dir einige Fragen stellen: Wie könnte ein Fehler zustande gekommen sein? Habe ich den Hörtext nicht richtig verstanden? Habe ich die Aufgaben nicht richtig verstanden?
- Höre dir gegebenenfalls den Hörtext mithilfe der Lösung noch einmal an. In diesem Fall solltest du diese Höraufgabe nach ein paar Tagen wiederholen.
- Versuche, mit der Bearbeitung jeder weiteren Hörverstehensaufgabe die Zahl der Hördurchgänge zu reduzieren, bis du bei der in der Prüfung üblichen Anzahl (zwei Mal) angelangt bist.

Die häufigsten Aufgabenformate in der Prüfung

Die folgenden Aufgabenformate kommen in der Abschlussprüfung besonders häufig vor:

Auswahlaufgabe *(Multiple choice)* mit Bildern

Bei diesem Aufgabentyp hörst du meist mehrere kurze Dialoge. Zu jedem dieser kurzen Hörtexte gibt es eine Aufgabe mit drei Bildern, von denen du das zum Hörtext passende Bild auswählen musst.

Beispiel

Text:

Tour guide: The tour starts at 9 am every Saturday and Sunday. The meeting point is in front of the train station.

Task and solution:

The tour starts at …

A ☐

B ☑

C ☐

Auswahlaufgabe *(Multiple choice)*

Hier bekommst du eine Frage mit verschiedenen Antworten vorgelegt, oder einen Satzanfang und mehrere Möglichkeiten, den Satz zu vervollständigen. Beachte, dass die Formulierung in der Aufgabe oft anders lautet als im Hörtext.

Beispiel

Text:

Tour guide: The tour starts at 9 am every Saturday and Sunday. The meeting point is in front of the train station.

Task and solution:

The tour starts at …

☐ 9 o'clock in the evening every Saturday.
☑ 9 o'clock in the morning every Saturday.
☐ 9 am every day.

Einsetzaufgabe *(Fill in the gap)*

Bei diesem Aufgabentyp geht es darum, Lücken in einer Tabelle zu vervollständigen. Manchmal musst du nur ein Wort, manchmal mehrere Wörter, und manchmal auch Zahlen eintragen. Wichtig ist, dass du dir die Aufgabenstellung vor dem Abspielen des Hörtextes gut durchliest, damit du weißt, auf welche Informationen du beim Zuhören besonders achten musst.

Beispiel

Text:

William: Yesterday, I went to a shop where I bought something to drink because I was thirsty. Then I went to the cinema and watched a movie.

Task and solution:

1	William went to the cinema to ____watch a movie____.

True or false?

Bei diesem Aufgabentyp sollst du entscheiden, ob eine Aussage richtig *(true)* oder falsch *(false)* ist. Meist weicht dabei die Formulierung der Aussage in der Aufgabenstellung etwas von derjenigen im Text ab.

Beispiel

Text:

William: Yesterday, I went to a shop where I bought something to drink because I was thirsty. Then I went to the cinema and watched a movie.

Task and solution:

	true	false
William bought something to eat because he was hungry.	☐	☑

1.2 Übungsaufgaben zum Kompetenzbereich „Listening“

Listening Comprehension Test 1: Short conversations

You are going to hear seven short recordings.
For each question there is a conversation to listen to and three pictures to look at. Tick (✓) the picture which answers the question.
Listen to the conversations twice.

1. Where does Tom want to go on holiday?

A ☐

B ☐

C ☐

2. What does the man need?

A ☐

B ☐

C ☐

3. How many minutes late is the train today?

A ☐

B ☐

C ☐

4. What did the bird take?

A ☐

B ☐

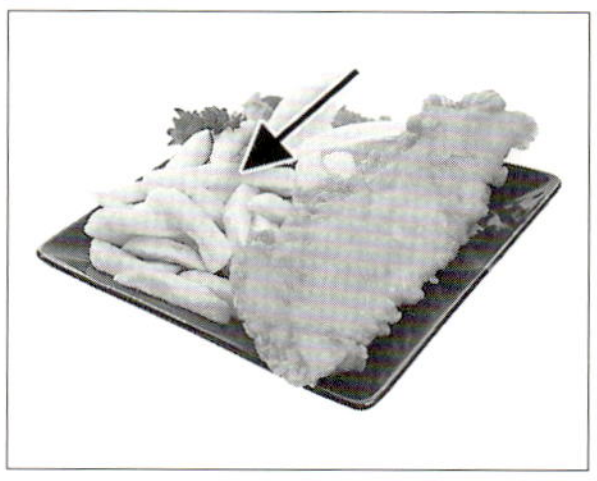
C ☐

5. Which question is difficult?

14	15	16
A ☐	B ☐	C ☐

6. What is Emma going to buy?

A ☐

B ☐

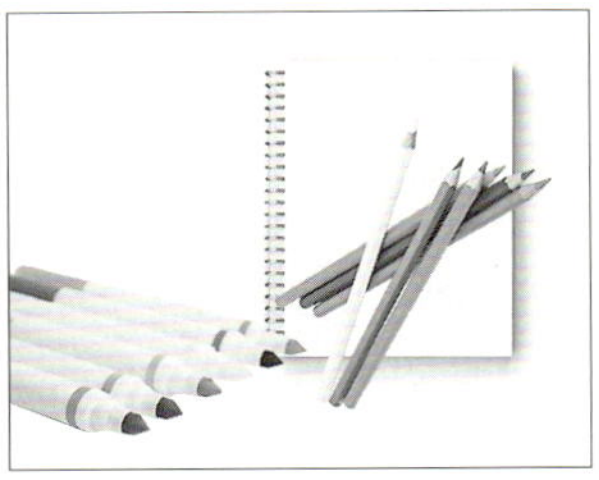
C ☐

7. Which way is lucky?

A ☐

B ☐

C ☐

Listening Comprehension Test 2: Stories from Yellowstone

Listen to the conversation between Greg and Sina about Yellowstone National Park. Tick (✓) the correct ending (A, B or C) to each statement (1–7).

Vocabulary:
stagecoach: *Postkutsche*

1. In Yellowstone National Park there are some animals …
   - A that are falsely called "buffalo". ☐
   - B that are very old. ☐
   - C that aren't friendly. ☐

2. In the summer, the hotels …
   - A are usually very full. ☐
   - B have parties every night. ☐
   - C do something very unusual. ☐

3. In Yellowstone there is always …
   - A a lot to do and see. ☐
   - B somewhere nice to walk. ☐
   - C a risk of snow. ☐

4. The second story is …
   - A more exciting than the first one. ☐
   - B about the Park's employees. ☐
   - C about the animals. ☐

5. Greg finds …
   - A Sina silly. ☐
   - B Yellowstone's attractions great. ☐
   - C the stories more interesting than the sights. ☐

6. The robbery happened in …
   - A 1904. ☐
   - B 1914. ☐
   - C 1940. ☐

7. The robber was …
   - A never found. ☐
   - B made up for visitors. ☐
   - C eventually caught. ☐

Listening Comprehension Test 3: Sharks

Listen to the conversation between Adam and Nicki about Nicki's experience of sharks. Tick (✓) the correct ending (A, B or C) to each statement (1–7).

1. Nicki's aim after leaving school was to …
   - A enjoy herself. ☐
   - B find a job abroad. ☐
   - C travel the world. ☐

2. Nicki found the shark research …
   - A through a group of people. ☐
   - B by reading about it. ☐
   - C on an advert in school. ☐

3. On her way to Florida, she …
   - A had to help someone. ☐
   - B tried to learn more about sharks. ☐
   - C thought more about her decision. ☐

4. Sharks sometimes attack because …
   - A people and seals often look the same to them. ☐
   - B surfboarders frighten them. ☐
   - C they're hungry and will eat anything. ☐

5. Shark attacks happen but only …
   - A in a few places in the world. ☐
   - B about 18 times every year. ☐
   - C a few people die from them. ☐

6. People are most at risk from …
   - A dogs. ☐
   - B crocodiles. ☐
   - C mosquitoes. ☐

7. The safest time to go into the sea in a shark area is …
   - A after breakfast. ☐
   - B about lunchtime. ☐
   - C after your evening meal. ☐

Listening Comprehension Test 4: Route 66

Listen to a report about Route 66 in the USA.
Complete the gaps (1–7) with information from the recording.

1	The highway is	________ km long.
2	The highway wasn't the first, the longest or the	________.
3	The dust storms happened during the	________.
4	The people who left wanted	________ life in California.
5	The 1940s and 50s saw the rise of the	________ culture.
6	The new highways were faster and didn't have many	________.
7	The places that suffered most were the	________.

Listening Comprehension Test 5: How 'chippies' began

Listen to a report about how fish and chips became a national dish in Britain. Complete the gaps (1–7) with information from the recording.

1	Americans like to eat	______________________.
2	Potatoes came to Britain in the	______________________.
3	Poor people ate chips because potatoes	______________________.
4	Fish and chips were first served together in the	______________________.
5	Fish and chips were often eaten on a	______________________.
6	Fresh fish could be bought everywhere because of the	______________________.
7	Today there are about	________________ chippies.

Listening Comprehension Test 6: A year in the USA

Lena has spent 12 months at a high school in Minnesota. Just before she returns to Germany, she is interviewed by a local radio station about her year in an American school.
Listen to the interview and decide if each sentence (1–7) is true or false.
Tick (✓) the correct box.

	In the interview, Lena says ...	true	false
1.	... at first it was difficult in the school.	☐	☐
2.	... the school wasn't very big.	☐	☐
3.	... every day was different in the school.	☐	☐
4.	... she played frisbee in the fall.	☐	☐
5.	... the whole school watched when the teams were playing.	☐	☐
6.	... all the doors into the school were locked.	☐	☐
7.	... her friends should go to America, too.	☐	☐

Listening Comprehension Test 7: Say no to plastic!

Lucy campaigns against plastic waste. Richard Gray from White Rose Radio has invited her into the studio to talk about the issue.
Listen to the interview and decide if each sentence (1–7) is true or false.
Tick (✓) the correct box.

Vocabulary: to decompose = *sich zersetzen, verwesen*

	In the radio show it is said that …	true	false
1.	… the beach wasn't very clean.	☐	☐
2.	… it takes hundreds of years for plastic to decompose.	☐	☐
3.	… the materials for the spoon came from China.	☐	☐
4.	… the spoon didn't have to travel very far.	☐	☐
5.	… in England plastic bags cost 50 pence.	☐	☐
6.	… many factories are being built to recycle the cups.	☐	☐
7.	… half a million paper cups are thrown away in England every day.	☐	☐
8.	… 99 % of paper cups can be recycled.	☐	☐
9.	… there are some plans to solve the problem already.	☐	☐

2 Kompetenzbereich: Reading

Es gibt viele verschiedene Arten von Lesetexten. Ebenso vielfältig können die Aufgabenstellungen dazu sein. Die Textsorten und Aufgabenstellungen, die am häufigsten in Klassenarbeiten und in Abschlussprüfungen vorkommen, werden wir dir hier vorstellen.

2.1 Strategien zum Kompetenzbereich „Reading"

Ganz gleich, welche Art von Lesetext oder Aufgabenstellung du bearbeiten musst, die Vorgehensweise ist dabei immer gleich.

Arbeitsschritt 1

Zunächst einmal ist es sinnvoll, sich den Text genau anzusehen. Manchmal kannst du bereits am **Layout**, d. h. an der Gestaltung, erkennen, um welche Textsorte es sich handelt. Wenn du weißt, ob der dir vorliegende Text eine Werbeanzeige, ein Zeitungsartikel oder ein Interview ist, dann bist du schon einen Schritt weiter.

Arbeitsschritt 2

Als Nächstes solltest du den **Text genau lesen**. Lies ihn erst einmal in Ruhe durch, um dir einen Überblick über den Inhalt zu verschaffen. Unbekannte Wörter kannst du im Wörterbuch nachschlagen. In der Prüfung darfst du auch ein Wörterbuch verwenden. Beachte jedoch, dass das Nachschlagen Zeit kostet und du zum Lösen der Aufgaben nicht jedes Wort kennen musst. Viele Wörter kannst du auch aus dem **Sinnzusammenhang erschließen**. Diese Fähigkeit kann man durch Üben verbessern.

Arbeitsschritt 3

Nun solltest du die **Aufgabenstellungen genau lesen**, damit du weißt, nach welchen Stellen du im Text suchen sollst. Wenn du nun den Lesetext ein zweites Mal liest, kannst du dabei ganz gezielt **Schlüsselwörter bzw. Textpassagen markieren**, damit du sie bei der Bearbeitung der Aufgaben schnell wiederfindest.

TIPP

- Versuche, beim ersten Lesen zu verstehen, worum es in dem Text geht.
- Lies den Text dann noch einmal genau durch. Du musst nicht alle Wörter kennen – einige kannst du auch durch den Sinnzusammenhang erschließen.
- Sieh dir die Aufgabenstellung genau an. Markiere beim nochmaligen Lesen des Textes Textstellen im Hinblick darauf, nach was in der Aufgabe gefragt wird.

Die häufigsten Aufgabenformate in der Prüfung

Die folgenden Aufgabenformate kommen in der Abschlussprüfung besonders häufig vor:

True or false?

Bei diesem Aufgabentyp erhältst du mehrere Aussagen *(statements)*. Du musst entscheiden, ob diese Aussagen im Vergleich mit der Information im Text richtig oder falsch sind *(true or false)*. Es kann auch vorkommen, dass du darüber hinaus die Belegstelle im Text angeben musst.

Beispiel

Text:

Yesterday, William went to a shop where he bought something to drink because he was thirsty. Then he went to the cinema and watched a movie.

Task and solution:

	true	false	line(s)
William went to a shop and bought something to eat.	☐	☑	1

Sehr hilfreich ist es, wenn du dir die Schlüsselwörter in der Aussage (hier z. B. „shop") und den Satzbau gut anschaust und dann im Text suchst. Oft gelingt es schnell, die passende Textstelle zu finden.

Auswahlaufgaben *(Multiple choice)*

Hier bekommst du eine Frage mit verschiedenen Antworten vorgelegt, oder einen Satzanfang und mehrere Möglichkeiten, den Satz zu vervollständigen.

Beispiel

Text:

The guided tour starts at 9 am every Saturday and Sunday. The meeting point is in front of the train station.

Tasks and solutions:

1. The tour starts at …
   a) ☐ 9 o'clock in the evening every Saturday.
   b) ☑ 9 o'clock in the morning every Saturday.
   c) ☐ 9 am every day.
2. Where does the tour start?
   a) ☐ next to the train station
   b) ☐ behind the train station
   c) ☑ in front of the train station

Lies die Aufgaben immer genau durch. Beachte, dass die Fragen bzw. Sätze oft anders formuliert sind als im Text, z. B. *9 o'clock in the morning* anstatt *9 am*. Versuche nun, die Antwort herauszufinden, die zum Text passt. Wenn du dir unsicher bist, dann probiere es andersherum: Schließe zuerst die Antworten aus, die falsch sind. Dann findest du vielleicht die richtige Antwort leichter. Die Reihenfolge der Fragen entspricht normalerweise dem Textaufbau, sodass du abschätzen kannst, wo im Text die Antwort stehen muss.

Zuordnungsaufgaben (*Matching*)

Bei diesem Aufgabenformat werden dir z. B. kurze Texte vorgegeben, die du einzelnen Personen zuordnen musst, zu denen diese passen. Meist sind mehr Kurztexte vorgegeben, als du brauchst. Lies dir die Texte genau durch und achte auf Schlüsselwörter, die dir einen Hinweis auf die richtige Zuordnung geben.

Beispiel

Text:

A Go on a ride on the London Eye! You will have a wonderful view of London.

B See where the Queen lives and visit Buckingham Palace.

C Relax in Hyde Park after an exciting day full of sightseeing.

D If you like shopping, Harrods is the place to be!

E Take part in a guided tour about London's history.

Task and solution:

Decide which of the sights or activities in London (A–D) is the most suitable for the people below.
Write the correct letters next to the numbers in the box.

1	*D*	*Melissa:* I love buying fashionable clothes.
2	*B*	*Pete:* I'm a fan of the Royal Family and would like to visit their palaces.
3	*C*	*Jenny:* I would like to rest a bit after a busy day of sightseeing.
4	*A*	*Tom:* Seeing London from above would be great.

Dir können aber auch Satzteile vorgegeben werden, die du jeweils mit dem zum Text passenden Satzende ergänzen musst. Auch hier werden dir meist mehr Möglichkeiten vorgegeben, als du brauchst.

Beispiel

Text:

The guided tour starts at 9 am every Saturday and Sunday. The meeting point is in front of the train station.

Task and solution:

Match the first parts of the sentences (1–2) with the sentence endings (A–C).

		A	starts at 9 o'clock in the evening.
1	The guided tour	B	meet at the station.
2	You	C	starts at 9 o'clock in the morning.

1.	2.
C	*B*

2.2 Übungsaufgaben zum Kompetenzbereich „Reading“

Reading Comprehension Test 1: Short texts

Read the adverts (A–D) and the statements (1–5). Decide whether the statements are **true** or **false**. Then tick (✓) the correct box.

A

SkyLine

Thank you for choosing to fly with **SkyLine**!

Aberdeen airport is small, but there is a large car park opposite the terminal. Cheap parking can be booked on our website.

Our planes to the Scottish islands are small. Only two bags are allowed for each person: one bag mustn't be more than 15 kilos and the other one not more than 5 kilos.

Have a safe flight!

B

Harry's closing down sale

Harry is closing his shop and everything must go!

Look at the offers:
- 30 % off all books
- 75 % off all T-shirts
- All CDs, vinyls, DVDs are half price.

Bring this advert with you, buy something for more than £ 25, and then Harry will give you an extra 10 % off everything!

Don't miss this fantastic offer!

C

Railton Hall Summer Party

Railton Hall's summer party starts on Friday at 9.00 p.m. and goes on through the night until Saturday – 24 hours of non-stop music and fun.

A huge number of bands come every year and this year, too. Bring all your friends!

Food and drink tents are on the festival field.

Tickets available from:
RailtonHall@festivals.co.uk

D

Cook for life!

OK – your mum or dad does it, your grandma, too. But can you?

Soon you'll be leaving school and getting a job. But one day you might not live at home, or your job might be in another town, or you might want your own flat. So, can you cook?

Join our 'Cook for life' course: 10 weeks every Thursday 6 p.m. – 9 p.m.

Come – cook – eat!!

Phone: 01652 / 56565

		true	false
1.	There are many car parks at Aberdeen airport.	☐	☐
2.	The music and fun is all weekend.	☐	☐
3.	The "Cook for life" course takes place only once.	☐	☐
4.	You can save the most money when you buy clothes.	☐	☐
5.	You can't take more than twenty kilos with you on the plane.	☐	☐

Reading Comprehension Test 2: More short texts

Read the adverts (A–D) and the statements (1–5). Decide whether the statements are **true** or **false**. Then tick (✓) the correct box.

A

YOUNG'S FITNESS STUDIO

Do you go jogging or cycling every day – even in winter when it's cold, dark and often wet?

No? Don't worry, you're not the only person. We have hundreds of members who were just like you! But now they're fit and healthy – so come to our fitness studio and meet some of them.

Join now for a 4-week trial period: **www.yfs.com**

B

We're looking for two students to work for four hours on Saturdays.
We do things for old people that they can't do any more; shopping or gardening, for example. Sometimes old people just need someone to talk to and have a cup of tea with! And, if you can drive, you can take an old person somewhere different for a few hours.
It's a fun Saturday job:
If you're interested, phone Sally on 01772/39742

C

Thorney Hotel

Weekend Special

Working hard?
Why not take a short break?

Thorney Hotel is 100 metres from a beautiful beach. We have a fantastic restaurant and large rooms and a great spa. We're only a 45-minute drive away from Norwich, where there is a theatre, cinemas and museums. There's something in the area for everyone!

www.Thorneyhotel@coastalhotels.com

D

FOR SALE

I love my car but I live in London now and don't need one. I have to sell it and I'm really sad about it. Can you give my car a nice new home?

2008, Mini: great condition, original, no damage, 85,000 miles, grey and black

If you are interested, email me and I'll send you a photo.

Jenny: jennyp@carsales.com

		true	false
1.	There is a special offer for Saturdays and Sundays at the hotel.	☐	☐
2.	Jenny needs a smaller car.	☐	☐
3.	You can write Sally an e-mail if you're interested in the job.	☐	☐
4.	The accommodation is 45-minutes away from the sea.	☐	☐
5.	A hundred people are members of the fitness studio.	☐	☐

Reading Comprehension Test 3: Cities

There are many great cities around the world. Read the information about some of them (A–H). Decide which city each person (1–5) likes. Write the correct letter into the box after each number. You can only use a letter once.

A	**Edinburgh** Take an umbrella! Scotland is often wet, but Edinburgh has lots to offer its visitors. There's a wonderful castle on top of a hill, nice shops, bagpipe players in the streets and much more. One great thing about the city is that the station is in the middle of it. In a few minutes you can be off your train and in the centre of Edinburgh.
B	**San Francisco** San Francisco isn't very hot even in summer but it's a fun city. You can see the Golden Gate Bridge, watch the seals playing in the harbour at Pier 39 or take a tour of the prison island, Alcatraz. But if you drive, take care – there are lots of very steep roads in the city.
C	**Paris** People find Paris romantic. It's got beautiful buildings, wide streets and open spaces. It's an elegant city with lots of museums and famous sights, such as the Eiffel Tower or Notre Dame Cathedral. You can take a boat tour on the River Seine or just sit in a street café and watch people.
D	**London** London is exciting and full of life. Everything you want is there: great theatres and museums, lots of shops and sights to see. It's also full of red double-decker buses and black taxis. Lots of famous people live in London, so maybe you'll see someone you know.
E	**Munich** Munich is a nice city to visit with lots of museums, art galleries, shops, parks and many other things. Of course, it's famous for its 'Oktoberfest' and its Christmas markets – and its football team. But there is one thing every visitor must try in Munich and that's 'Weißwürste'!
F	**New York** New York is famous for its skyscrapers, the Statue of Liberty, yellow taxis and Central Park. But there is much more to see and do in New York, including a Broadway play in the evening. New York's nickname is 'The Big Apple' but no one really knows why it's called that!
G	**Rome** Pizza, pasta and ice cream. Rome has it all and the original versions! Of course, there is more to Rome than food. Around every street corner there is an ancient building. Walk where Julius Caesar walked or visit the Colosseum where huge crowds watched gladiators fight – and if you get tired of all of Rome's history then go shopping!
H	**Barcelona** Barcelona has a great football team! But there is much more to the city than just sport. It's elegant with many beautiful buildings and an amazing cathedral. It's also got beaches and a cool harbour where lots of rich people have their expensive boats. Barcelona is always worth a visit.

1. ☐

Lilly: I like history and so I come here a lot. Every time I visit the city, I see something new – I mean old, but new for me. There's another reason I like coming here: the food is great – far better than what I get at home.

2. ☐

Kathy: I don't like lots of sun or flying very far, so I often get on a train and go there – and I know I won't need my sun cream or my passport! I enjoy the atmosphere and the sounds of the city. It's a great place to visit for weekends.

3. ☐

Simon: I like to go far away from England. When you're young, you should explore the world. What I like about here is not only the famous sights and the high-rise buildings, but that there is always lots to do during the day and in the evening – and everyone speaks English!

4. ☐

Jamal: When I go somewhere, I want the city to have lots of different things in it. I don't just want theatres and sights. I love this city because it has everything: I can go sightseeing in the morning, swimming in the sea in the afternoon and maybe even watch a football match in the evening.

5. ☐

Charlie: The weather in this city is not always pleasant, but it can be nice and warm there in summer. I like all the attractions the city has and sometimes I visit it in the autumn and winter for the special events – and I can also eat something that I can't eat at home.

Reading Comprehension Test 4: Jobs

Read the information about the jobs (A–H) and about the people who do them (1–5). Match each job to a person and write the letter (A–H) into the box next to their name. You can only use a letter once.

A	**Architect** Architects usually design houses but sometimes they work on special projects, too, for example changing a factory into flats for senior citizens. They work with builders, gardeners and lots of other people. They have to be creative but also design what people want.
B	**Teacher** Many people think teachers have a lot of holidays and free time but they don't. They have marking to do and a lot of preparing, too. The job is exciting because it's about young people and helping them to become adults and to get good jobs.
C	**Bus driver** There are two types of drivers: the ones who work in and around towns and cities and others that take people on trips or on holidays. It's a very responsible job because drivers have a lot of rules to obey and they are also looking after a lot of people and even money.
D	**Team assistant** Team assistants have to do many things and every day is different. They need to be able to use a computer, write well, and have a nice telephone voice. Most team assistants have contact with people in their company and with visitors.
E	**Shop assistant** There are different types of shop assistant. Some work in supermarkets and others in clothes shops, for example. They need to be friendly and enjoy helping customers. Some assistants deal with money and others make the shop windows look nice, so there are always lots of things to do.
F	**Pilot** Everyone thinks this job is great and pilots see a lot of countries around the world. Flying is fun but they don't really see the countries they fly to – they often just see the airports. Pilots have to look after their passengers and make sure they get to where they are going safely and on time.
G	**Hairdresser** Hairdressers deal with lots of different people. Young people often like to be fashionable – so hairdressers must be able to do lots of exciting styles and colours. Older people aren't that keen to experiment, they just want to look nice but have the same style. Hairdressers also need to be sociable and be able to have a chat with their customers.
H	**Policeman/woman** Every day is different for the police – sometimes they go to an accident or sometimes they are working with football fans. They don't all drive cars with blue lights and sirens! And their job isn't like the programmes on television or action films. They deal with people, some of which are nice and some aren't.

1. ☐  **Eva:** A lot of people think my job is cool, especially because a woman is doing it! I don't work in an office and I go to lots of different countries but I don't often stay in one for a long time: sometimes just for one or two hours.

2. ☐  **Tom:** I like being creative. I love it when young people come to me and ask me to make them look stylish. Older people, on the other hand, aren't very adventurous about new styles. I usually talk a lot to my customers, too.

3. ☐  **Harry:** I like working with people and going to different places. Sometimes I'm away from home for a week or more. One week I might be in France and then have a few days at home and then I might be in Scotland.

4. ☐  **Kim:** What I want to do is not always what my customers want. I'm very creative and I like having a task where I can try out different ideas. I often see something in a town or city and think, 'Wow, that's got a great shape – I could really do something with that!'

5. ☐  **Amy:** The first thing I have to do every morning is make coffee! But then the day starts. I have lots of emails to look at and messages to deal with. Sometimes it's very busy and everyone wants me to do things at the same time – but that's part of the job.

Reading Comprehension Test 5: The mystery of the Mary Celeste

Read the following story. Then match the first parts of the sentences (1–8) with the sentence endings (A–I).

The mystery of the Mary Celeste

What happened to the ship called the Mary Celeste? People have been trying to answer this question for more than 100 years. The Mary Celeste was a sailing ship. It was carrying 1,701 barrels of industrial alcohol – not the type of alcohol you drink. It was going from New York to Genoa in Italy. There were seven sailors, the captain, his wife and their two-year-old daughter on board. All the men were good sailors and had a lot of experience. They sailed from New York on 7th November, 1872.

On 4th December, between the coast of Portugal and a group of islands in the Atlantic Ocean, another ship saw the Mary Celeste coming towards it in a strange way. The captain sent two of his men to climb onto the Mary Celeste to see what was wrong. They did, but there was no one on it.

There were more surprises, too: the alcohol was still there, there weren't any signs of a fight, there was a lot of food, and the crew's belongings were still there, too – only the lifeboat was missing, and the ship's papers and navigational instruments. The sails were in bad condition, and there was some water inside the ship, but it was not seriously damaged. The ship's diary had been completed every day until 25th November, nine days earlier.

The men who found the ship sailed to Gibraltar in it and left it there. The captain of the Mary Celeste, his family and his men have never been found. What happened to them and why they got off the ship is still a mystery.

		A	in the autumn.
1	No one knows	B	was found by another ship.
2	When the ship left,	C	heavily damaged.
3	All the men on the ship had	D	the true story.
4	The Mary Celeste left America	E	taken their personal things with them.
5	The Mary Celeste	F	was found on 25th November, 1872.
6	There was nobody	G	sailed many times before.
7	No one had	H	on the ship when it was found.
8	The ship was not	I	there were ten people on it.

1.	2.	3.	4.	5.	6.	7.	8.

Reading Comprehension Test 6: The polar bear problem

Polar bears are in danger because of global warming. Read the story and find out why. Match the first part of each sentence (1–8) to the correct ending (A–J). There are two endings not used.

The polar bear problem

Canada has got a lot of polar bears. They like to hunt seals on the ice of Hudson Bay. Thirty years ago, ice was on the sea from October to June but today it is often only there from December to May.

Polar bears can only hunt the seals from the ice. They also have to eat a lot of them to gain fat because in the summer they live on the land where there isn't much food for them. The polar bears used to hunt for more than eight months every year, now they are lucky if they can hunt for six months on the ice. A hungry bear is not a happy bear – and for the people in a town called Churchill, hungry bears are a big problem.

The bears always came to Churchill in late October to wait for the ice to start and they weren't a problem. Now they come early in July! And, because they are hungry they are now coming close to people's homes where they look for things to eat in bins or they attack dogs. But a polar bear will attack a person, too. No one locks their car here; if a bear chases you, you can get into anyone's car, lock the door and you're safe.

Churchill has a special polar bear prison and polar bear police. If a bear is a problem, the polar bear police catch it and take it to the 'prison'. When there is some ice, the polar bear is taken by helicopter and put onto the ice so it can hunt and be happy once again.

		A	have changed.
1	Polar bears	B	get hungry.
2	The times when bears can find food	C	help the bears.
3	In summer, polar bears	D	find a polar bear outside your house.
4	The polar bears have become	E	leave their car doors open.
5	The bears are coming	F	break into houses.
6	In Churchill, you might	G	a problem.
7	The people in Churchill	H	live on the land in winter.
8	People try to	I	hunt seals when the sea is frozen.
		J	into town much earlier now.

1.	2.	3.	4.	5.	6.	7.	8.

Reading Comprehension Test 7: Just another day at work

Read the true story of a plane that landed in the Hudson River, New York.
Tick (✓) the correct ending (A, B or C) to each statement (1–7).
There is only <u>one</u> ending for each statement.

Just another day at work

1 On 15th January, 2009, Captain Chesley Sullenberger and his crew got the plane ready for its flight. It was a full plane with 150 passengers on it going to Charlotte in North Carolina. It was a cold but clear day and everything was normal at first as the plane took off from LaGuardia, one of New York's airports. It climbed into the sky as usual, but suddenly at about 3,000 feet, the plane hit a lot of birds – big Canadian geese.

The birds went into the engines and both of them stopped working. The captain tried to start the engines again but they wouldn't. Sullenberger told LaGuardia airport what the problem was but he didn't have the height or the power to return to it. He was told to try Teterboro airport, an airport that was also quite near, but the captain said he was unable to reach it. All this time the plane was flying with no power and slowly losing its height.

The only chance Sullenberger had was to land the plane in the Hudson River. He only had time to issue the command 'Brace for impact' – meaning the passengers had to put their heads down and get ready to crash. Just about six minutes from taking off, the plane landed in the river.

The doors of the plane were opened and everyone got out: most of them stood on the wings or the evacuation slides. Slowly the water came into the plane and it began to sink. The passengers on the wings stayed there but they were now standing in the freezing water.

Lots of boats saw the plane land in the river and went to help. The first boats got to the plane in only a few minutes and most of the passengers could get on them. Other boats picked up the rest of the passengers.

Two things were amazing: first, no one died in the accident and, secondly, only four planes have ever landed safely on water before.

1. The captain made sure the plane was …
   A ☐ full of passengers.
   B ☐ going to South Carolina.
   C ☐ okay to fly.
2. The flight …
   A ☐ was delayed by 30 minutes.
   B ☐ started just like any other flight.
   C ☐ started with a few problems.
3. The geese …
   A ☐ passed the plane.
   B ☐ just touched the plane a bit.
   C ☐ badly damaged the plane.
4. The pilot …
   A ☐ tried to land at a different airport.
   B ☐ knew he could not get to the other airport.
   C ☐ knew he could start the engines again.
5. The captain …
   A ☐ explained the problem to the passengers.
   B ☐ told the passengers what to do.
   C ☐ didn't have time to tell the passengers what to do.
6. All the passengers …
   A ☐ went onto the wings of the plane.
   B ☐ had to jump into the freezing water.
   C ☐ got out of the plane safely.
7. The passengers were picked up …
   A ☐ very quickly.
   B ☐ slowly.
   C ☐ all together.

Chesley Sullenberger

Reading Comprehension Test 8: Pacific Coast tsunamis

Read the text about tsunamis along the Pacific Coast of America.
Tick (✓) the correct ending (A, B or C) to each statement (1–7).
There is only one ending for each statement.

Pacific Coast tsunamis

Storms make big waves and sometimes these waves can do a lot of damage. On the west coast of North America there is another reason why high waves can happen – tsunamis. Crescent City in California, for example, has had more than 30 tsunamis since 1933, so it's important to know when one is coming and also what to do.

Tsunamis often happen because there is an earthquake under the sea. When the waves from the earthquake get near the coast, they get bigger. The tsunami waves are usually between 6–18 metres high but some have been as high as 30 metres.

There are two types of tsunami: a local one and a distant one. If an earthquake happens near the coast, then it's a local tsunami. The waves from a local tsunami can start very soon after the ground has stopped shaking – sometimes only fifteen minutes later – and they are usually the biggest ones.

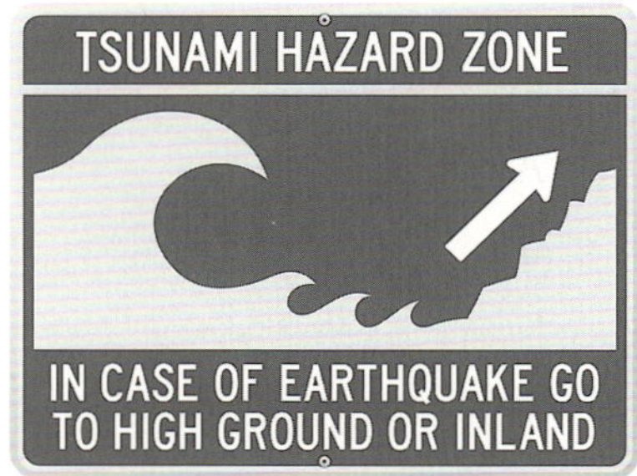

A distant tsunami is when the earthquake is far away under the ocean. These tsunami waves are usually smaller and take many hours to reach the coast.

It's recommended that every house has a tsunami emergency kit. In it people should, for example, have food and water for three days, a tent, sleeping bags, warm clothes, money and other items like a radio and a torch.

If people feel an earthquake or notice that the sea is receding, or if they are warned that a tsunami is on its way to the coast, they must go to one of the high safe areas and stay there. There are signs which show people where to go. A tsunami isn't just one wave – there can be many waves and the danger can last for hours. The waves can also go up rivers, so people who live near a river also have to go to a high place.

When the danger is over, a message is sent over the radio and the police tell people in the safe areas that they can return home.

1. The Pacific Coast …
   - A ☐ is known for bad storms.
   - B ☐ is known as a tsunami area.
   - C ☐ has been known as a dangerous one since 1933.

2. One part of California has …
   - A ☐ never had a tsunami.
   - B ☐ seen many tsunamis.
   - C ☐ had a tsunami every 34 years.

3. After an underwater earthquake near land, the waves …
   A ☐ can continue all day.
   B ☐ are usually small.
   C ☐ can come very quickly.

4. The earthquakes under the sea which are less dangerous for the people living on the coast are those …
   A ☐ a long way from the beach.
   B ☐ that only last for 15 minutes.
   C ☐ near the coast.

5. People in the area …
   A ☐ shouldn't leave their houses.
   B ☐ shouldn't live near the sea.
   C ☐ should always be ready to leave their homes.

6. Everyone along the coast knows …
   A ☐ where they can be safe.
   B ☐ where they can buy emergency kits.
   C ☐ the police will help them.

7. The tsunami warnings are …
   A ☐ only for the people living at the coast.
   B ☐ for people living near rivers, too.
   C ☐ in many different languages.

Reading Comprehension Test 9: Green roofs benefit people

Decide if each sentence is true or false and where you find the information in the text. Then tick (✓) the correct box and give the lines where you find the information. Both parts of the answer must be correct.

Green roofs benefit people

Water is a necessity of life. Rain, especially, helps plants grow and stay green. But too much rain – especially in cities – can lead to flooding. That can cause waste water systems, like sewers, to overflow and send pollutants into rivers and other waterways. To fight the problem, several cities in the United States are starting programs like rooftop gardens. […]

A team at the University of the District of Columbia in the nation's capital has created a garden on the top of one school building. The garden holds many kinds of plants to help absorb rainwater … and grow food at the same time. […] Rainwater is collected in large containers and sent through a system that waters the rooftop garden. The roof is filled with green life that appeals to insects. […]

A rooftop garden

In cities, "you don't have that many spaces to choose from and so rooftops are just (unused) space," says Caitlin Arlotta. She is a student in the school's Urban Agriculture program. The project is part of a research program to see which plants do well on rooftops. The researchers are looking at plants including strawberries, tomatoes and sweet potatoes. "We have the same experiment running with tomatoes as we do with strawberries, so we're doing variety trials and we're trying just to see which variety grows the best in a green roof setting." [...]

One goal of the program is food justice; or in Arlotta's words, "bringing fresh food into cities where you wouldn't necessarily have that access." And that includes produce that might be more used by immigrants. "In the U.S., it may not seem very common to use hibiscus leaves and sweet potato leaves as food, but in many places around the world it is." [...]

Sandy Farber Bandier helps run UDC's Master Gardener program. It seeks to improve cities and make them beautiful by training people to become Master Gardeners. She says she's been surprised by the garden's output. "My biggest surprise was that we produced 4,250 pounds of produce the first year and were able to give that to people in need." [...]

She likes being able to show people who live in D.C. and others beyond the nation's capital what – and how – food can be grown on a rooftop. "This is the future for food." [...]

Abridged and adapted from: Julie Taboh, Susan Shand and Caty Weaver: Green roofs benefit people, in: Voice of America Learning English

		true	false	line(s)
1.	In the cities, too little rain can cause problems.	☐	☐	______
2.	The plants in the rooftop garden soak up the rainwater.	☐	☐	______
3.	Rainwater cannot be used to grow food in the garden because it is polluted.	☐	☐	______
4.	Animals are attracted by the plants in the rooftop garden.	☐	☐	______
5.	The researchers try to find out what plants grow best on the rooftop.	☐	☐	______
6.	They only want to grow food that is commonly eaten in the United States.	☐	☐	______
7.	Ms Farber Bandier was happy with the amount of food produced in the garden.	☐	☐	______

3 Kompetenzbereich: Mediating

Im Englischunterricht sollst du u. a. auf typische Alltagssituationen vorbereitet werden, in denen du Englisch benötigst. Folgende Situationen können dir so oder so ähnlich tatsächlich passieren:

- Du machst Urlaub in einem englischsprachigen Land und musst dich in verschiedensten Situationen verständigen (z. B. im Restaurant, im Supermarkt, beim Bäcker, im Hotel oder auf der Straße).
- Du hast Besuch (z. B. aus England oder den USA), der nur Englisch spricht. Dein Besuch trifft beispielsweise deine Großmutter, die nur Deutsch kann. Weil du beide Sprachen sprichst, wirst du gebeten zu dolmetschen.
- Dein englischer oder amerikanischer Freund schreibt dir auf Englisch, oder du liest z. B. einen englischen Text im Internet, und dein kleiner Bruder stellt dir Fragen zum Inhalt, die du ihm auf Deutsch beantworten sollst.
- Du machst Urlaub mit deiner Familie und deine Eltern können nicht so gut Englisch. Ihr lernt jemanden kennen, der nur Englisch spricht – und wieder wirst du gebeten zu dolmetschen.
- Im gleichen Urlaub seht ihr eine Speisekarte oder ein Hinweisschild, und dein Vater möchte wissen, was dort auf Englisch geschrieben steht. Also erklärst du es ihm auf Deutsch.

3.1 Strategien zum Kompetenzbereich „Mediating"

Aufgaben zum Kompetenzbereich „Mediating" stellen genau solche Situationen nach. Du bist derjenige, der vermittelt bzw. dolmetscht. Diesen Tipp solltest du dabei beherzigen:

TIPP

Es geht in einer Sprachmittlungsaufgabe nicht darum, den Text oder das Gesagte immer Wort für Wort zu übersetzen. Vielmehr sollst du den **Kern der Aussage** wiedergeben, und zwar so, wie du dich in der entsprechenden Situation ausdrücken würdest.

Manchmal kannst du aber auch einfach übersetzen, was du hörst oder liest. Wenn du beispielsweise ein Schild siehst, auf dem *Toilets are in the basement* steht, kannst du wortwörtlich übersetzen mit „Die Toiletten sind im Keller". Wenn du aber beispielsweise *Keep off the grass!* wortwörtlich mit „Halte dich fern vom Rasen" übersetzt, hört sich das im Deutschen seltsam an. Also formulierst du um zu „Das Betreten des ist Rasens verboten". Auch möglich ist „Man darf nicht auf den Rasen (gehen)" oder „Es ist verboten, den Rasen zu betreten" oder „Hier steht, dass man den Rasen nicht betreten darf".
Wenn du in einem Gespräch vermittelst und dein englischer Freund sagt: "I'm interested in football. I would really like to go to a match while I'm in Germany!", dann könntest du für deine Oma übersetzen: „Er interessiert sich für Fuß-

ball und möchte gern zu einem Spiel gehen, während er in Deutschland ist" oder „Er sagt, dass er sich für Fußball interessiert und dass er sehr gern zu einem Fußballspiel gehen würde, während er hier ist". Wichtig ist, dass du nicht in der Ich-Form bleibst, sondern einen **Perspektivwechsel** zur 3. Person Singular vornimmst: „Er sagt, dass er sich für Fußball interessiert" und nicht „Ich interessiere mich für Fußball".
Wichtig für das Dolmetschen in die Fremdsprache ist außerdem, dass du dir bestimmte Redewendungen und Schildaufschriften im Laufe der Zeit einprägst. Würdest du „Wie alt bist du?" mit "What is your age?" statt mit "How old are you?" und „Rasen betreten verboten" mit "Stepping on the lawn forbidden" statt mit der festen Wendung "Keep off the grass" übersetzen, dann würde man dich zwar verstehen, aber die volle Punktzahl könntest du damit in einer Prüfung nicht erreichen, da ein englischer Muttersprachler sich nicht so ausdrücken würde.

TIPP

- Oft ist die wortwörtliche Übersetzung nicht passend. Übertrage vielmehr den Kern bzw. Sinn der Aussage in die andere Sprache.
- Überlege, ob du beim Übertragen von wörtlicher Rede statt der Ich- oder Wir-Form die Personalformen der 3. Person Singular (er/sie/es) oder Plural (sie) nehmen musst; du kannst manchmal auch das unpersönliche „man" verwenden (z. B. „Man darf den Rasen nicht betreten").
- Oft kannst du den Satz mit „Er/Sie sagt/schreibt, dass …" oder mit „Hier steht, dass …" beginnen
- Präge dir möglichst viele Redewendungen und typische Schildaufschriften ein.

In den folgenden „Mediating exercises" trainierst du erst einmal, wie du dich in bestimmten Situationen auf Englisch ausdrückst. Überlege dir, was du auf Deutsch sagen würdest, und versuche, den Satz sinngemäß ins Englische zu übertragen. Achte auch darauf, dass man sich im Englischen meist etwas höflicher ausdrückt als im Deutschen. Verwende dabei Wörter und Wendungen wie „please", „Could / May I …" etc.
In den darauffolgenden Aufgaben bekommst du Schilder und Gebrauchstexte vorgelegt, die in eine Situation eingebettet sind. Du wirst dabei auf Englisch oder Deutsch aufgefordert, bestimmte Informationen in die jeweils andere Sprache zu übertragen. Auch hier gilt, dass sich nicht immer alles Wort für Wort übertragen lässt. Wichtig ist, dass die wesentlichen Informationen vom Empfänger verstanden werden.

3.2 Übungsaufgaben zum Kompetenzbereich „Mediating“

Mediating exercise 1

1. What do you say in English?

a) *In der Stadt:*
Du fragst nach dem Weg zur nächsten Bushaltestelle.

b) *Im Restaurant:*
Du möchtest gerne die Speisekarte haben.

c) *Im Jeansladen:*
Du fragst, ob es die Jeans noch eine Nummer größer gibt.

d) *Du sitzt mit deinen Freunden im Café.*
Du möchtest wissen, was sie am Wochenende gemacht haben.

e) *Du telefonierst mit deiner besten Freundin.*
Du kommst nicht mit ins Kino, weil du krank bist.

f) *Dein Bus hat Verspätung. Du rufst deinen Freund an, mit dem du verabredet bist.*
Du wirst dich ein wenig verspäten.

g) *Auf einer Party:* Deine Freundin sagt, ihr gefällt die Party. Stimme ihr zu.

h) *Nach der Schule:*
Schlage vor, ins Kino zu gehen.

2. Du bist mit deiner Familie in den USA. Dein kleiner Bruder versteht noch kein Englisch, also erklärst du ihm, was auf den Schildern steht.

a) **No dog waste on grass!**

b) 

c) 

Keep off the ice! Drowning hazard.
Ice may break.

d) 

3. Your British friend Sam has come to Germany with his family. He only speaks English and can't read the following signs. Explain them to your friend in English.

a) **Bitte nicht stören!**

b) **Rauchen lässt Ihre Haut altern!**

c)

d)

4. Du bist mit deiner Familie gerade in der Nähe von Boston. Dein kleiner Bruder sieht am 14. Oktober folgendes Plakat und möchte wissen, was darauf steht. Beantworte seine Fragen auf Deutsch.

Bruder: Auf dem Plakat steht etwas von einem Fest, oder? Was ist das für ein Fest?

Du: ______________________________

____

____

Bruder: Wann findet es statt? Vielleicht können wir hingehen.

Du: ______________________________

____

____

Bruder: Das würde ja klappen. Was gibt es denn auf dem Fest?

Du: ______________________________

____

____

____

Bruder: Klingt gut. Muss man denn für den Eintritt zahlen?

Du: ______________________________

____

Mediating exercise 2

1. What do you say in the following situations? Find the English phrase.

   a) *In der Schule: Es ist heiß im Klassenzimmer.*
   Du fragst höflich, ob du das Fenster öffnen darfst.

   ____

   b) *In der Mathestunde:*
   Bitte deinen Nachbarn, dir einen Stift zu leihen.

   ____

   c) *Nach der Englischarbeit:*
   Sage, dass die Prüfung schwierig war.

   ____

   d) *Nach der Schule:*
   Frage, ob dir jemand bei den Hausaufgaben helfen kann.

   ____

   e) *Im Einkaufszentrum:*
   Die Verkäuferin fragt dich, wonach du suchst.

   ____

f) Die Verkäuferin fragt, ob dir der Pullover passt.

____

g) *(Jemand bedankt sich.)* Du erwiderst: „Bitte schön."

____

2. Du bist mit deiner Großmutter in Australien. Deine Oma kann nicht so gut Englisch, deshalb erklärst du ihr, was auf den folgenden Schildern steht.

a) **Do not feed the alligators!**

b) **YOU ARE NOW IN A WIFI AREA**

c) **Cattle crossing – Please drive slowly!**

d) **Attention!**
AGGRESSIVE BEES!

When attacked:

- Run.
- Get inside a building or vehicle.
- Cover mouth and nose.
- Don't swat the bees.
- Don't panic.

First aid kits and emergency phones in emergency tents every 500 metres.

3. During your holiday in England you made a new friend – Julie. A few weeks later, she comes to Germany to visit you. She only speaks English and does not understand the following signs. Explain them to her in English.

a)

b)

Betreten der Baustelle verboten

Eltern haften für ihre Kinder

c)

d)

Das Jugendschutzgesetz verbietet den Verkauf von

- Alcopops und Spirituosen an unter 18-jährige
- Wein und Bier an unter 16-jährige

Das Personal darf einen Ausweis verlangen!

4. Du bist mit deinen Eltern in Cornwall. Ihr wollt heute nicht im Hotel, sondern auswärts frühstücken. Deine Eltern, die nicht so gut Englisch sprechen, wollen wissen, was auf der folgenden Tafel steht. Beantworte ihre Fragen auf Deutsch.

a) „Breakfast" heißt doch „Frühstück", oder? Was wird denn angeboten und wieviel kostet es jeweils?

b) Das ist alles? Gibt es noch mehr?

c) Sind wir denn noch rechtzeitig dran? Bis wann gibt es denn Frühstück?

d) Heute ist so ein schöner Tag. Vielleicht können wir das Frühstück auch mitnehmen und im Park essen. Geht das?

Mediating exercise 3

1. You are in New York. What would you say in the following situations?

a) *Du bist in Manhattan.*
Frage einen Passanten höflich nach dem Weg zum Empire State Building.

b) *Der Passant spricht zu schnell.*
Sage, dass du ihn nicht verstanden hast.

c) *Nach der Besichtigung gehst du in ein Café.*
Du bestellst eine heiße Schokolade.

d) *Du kommst mit einem netten jungen Paar ins Gespräch.*
Du erzählst ihnen, dass du am Abend wieder nach Deutschland fliegst.

e) Frage die beiden, ob sie schon einmal in Deutschland waren.

f) Sie verneinen, wollen aber gerne einmal dorthin.

2. In den Sommerferien darfst du mit einem Freund und seiner Familie in die USA. Die kleine Schwester deines Freundes kann noch kein Englisch und möchte wissen, was auf den folgenden Schildern steht. Antworte ihr auf Deutsch.

a) Leave this bathroom clean for the next user!

b)

c)
Reserve ticket:
Ferry to Liberty Island and Ellis Island:

Adults	$ 25.50
Children (4–12)	$ 16.00
Seniors (62+)	$ 21.00

Ferry access to the grounds of the Statue of Liberty, plus the Ellis Island Immigration Museum.

d)

3. You are back in Germany and Brandon, an American exchange student, is staying with you and your family. Brandon speaks only a little bit of German, so you tell him what the following signs say.

a) 

b) LEERE FLASCHEN BITTE IN DEN CONTAINER WERFEN!

c) Aufzug außer Betrieb!

d) NUR IM NOTFALL ÖFFNEN! DIE TÜR IST ALARMGESICHERT!

4. You would like to do a tour of Hamburg harbour with Brandon, and you have found the following information on the internet. Answer Brandon's questions about the tour in English.

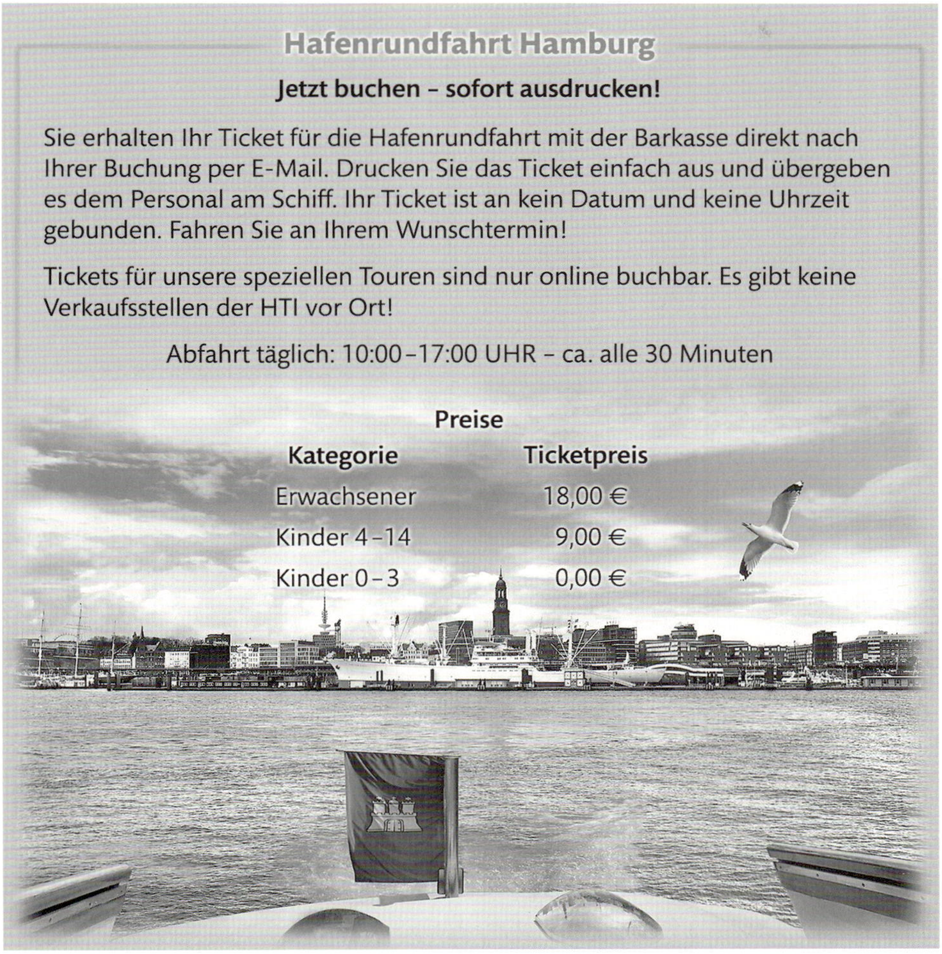

Hafenrundfahrt Hamburg

Jetzt buchen – sofort ausdrucken!

Sie erhalten Ihr Ticket für die Hafenrundfahrt mit der Barkasse direkt nach Ihrer Buchung per E-Mail. Drucken Sie das Ticket einfach aus und übergeben es dem Personal am Schiff. Ihr Ticket ist an kein Datum und keine Uhrzeit gebunden. Fahren Sie an Ihrem Wunschtermin!

Tickets für unsere speziellen Touren sind nur online buchbar. Es gibt keine Verkaufsstellen der HTI vor Ort!

Abfahrt täglich: 10:00–17:00 UHR – ca. alle 30 Minuten

Preise

Kategorie	Ticketpreis
Erwachsener	18,00 €
Kinder 4–14	9,00 €
Kinder 0–3	0,00 €

eigene Darstellung nach https://hamburgtourist.info/hafenrundfahrten/hafenrundfahrt-barkasse-speicherstadt.html

a) A harbor tour sounds great! Where can we get the tickets?

____

____

____

b) Do we have to decide when we want to go?

____

____

____

c) When do the tours take place?

____

____

____

d) I've just turned 16. Do I still get a discount?

e) Do they say what we can see on the tour?

4 Kompetenzbereich: Writing

Viele Schülerinnen und Schüler sind der Meinung, dass sie sich auf den Bereich „Writing“ nicht vorbereiten können, weil viel von der individuellen Einschätzung der Lehrkraft abhängt. Erschwerend kommen im Fach Englisch noch die Fremdsprache und die damit verbundenen Fehler hinzu. Aus diesen Gründen beschäftigen sich viele im Vorfeld einer Prüfung gar nicht erst mit diesem Kompetenzbereich, ohne zu bedenken, dass er in der Regel ein Viertel der Note in der schriftlichen Prüfung ausmacht.
Mache nicht den gleichen Fehler und lies die folgenden Seiten gut durch. Du wirst sehen: Eine sinnvolle und erfolgreiche Vorbereitung auf das Verfassen englischer Texte ist möglich.

4.1 Strategien zum Kompetenzbereich „Writing“

Auf die Textproduktion in Klassenarbeiten und Prüfungen kannst du dich nur langfristig gut vorbereiten. Wenn du dir erst zwei Tage vor der Prüfung überlegst, dass du in diesem Bereich noch Schwächen hast, dann ist das für eine sinnvolle Vorbereitung zu spät.
Anhand der Schreibaufgaben in diesem Buch übst du Schritt für Schritt das eigenständige Formulieren, das du für den Prüfungsteil *Writing* benötigst. Ganz gleich, welche Art von Text du schreiben musst, die Vorgehensweise ist dabei immer dieselbe:

- In der Prüfung musst du zwischen zwei Aufgabensets wählen. Jedes Set beinhaltet zwei Schreibaufgaben. Der Schwierigkeitsgrad ist derselbe, aber vielleicht fällt dir zu einem Thema mehr ein als zu dem anderen, oder du schreibst lieber eine persönliche Nachricht an einen Freund als eine kurze Bewerbung. Um auf die Prüfung gut vorbereitet zu sein, solltest du aber alle Übungsaufgaben in diesem Buch bearbeiten. Arbeitsschritt 1
- Bevor du einen Text schreibst, lies die Aufgabenstellung gut durch und überlege, was darin von dir verlangt wird. Erhältst du mit der Aufgabenstellung irgendwelche Vorgaben, die du in deinen Text einbringen musst? (z. B. eine Ausgangssituation, Stichwörter, ein oder mehrere Bilder)? Vielleicht hilft es dir, die Informationen, die dein Text enthalten soll, in der Aufgabenstellung zu unterstreichen. Oder sollst du einen „freien“ Text ohne Vorgaben schreiben? Arbeitsschritt 2
  Wenn du eine E-Mail verfassen sollst, überlege dir, wer der Empfänger/die Empfängerin ist und wie du mit ihm/ihr sprechen würdest. In einer Nachricht an einen Freund/eine Freundin verwendest du eine andere Anrede und eine andere Abschiedsfloskel als z. B. in einem Bewerbungsschreiben (siehe auch unter „Hilfreiche Wendungen zur Textproduktion, S. 47 ff.).

Arbeitsschritt 3

- Es kann hilfreich sein, wenn du dir vor dem Ausarbeiten deines Textes Stichpunkte notierst, die du später ausformulierst. Beachte dabei genau die Vorgaben in der Aufgabenstellung (z. B. in Form von Bildern oder Stichworten) und überlege dann, was du noch hinzufügen musst. Wenn es dir hilft, halte deine Gedanken in einer Mindmap fest. So kannst du sie strukturieren.

Arbeitsschritt 4

- Arbeite nun den Text aus. Achte dabei darauf, dass er verständlich geschrieben und logisch aufgebaut ist. Greife in deinem Text auf passende Redewendungen zurück, die du gelernt hast. Schreibe aber nicht zu lange Sätze – so kannst du Grammatikfehlern leichter vorbeugen. Beim Schreiben von Texten kommt es vielmehr darauf an, dass du die von dir verfassten Sätze sprachlich variieren kannst, denn dauernde Wiederholungen wirken ermüdend. Außerdem ist es wichtig, die einzelnen Sätze miteinander zu verknüpfen, um Zusammenhänge oder Folgen zu verdeutlichen. Diese Verknüpfungen können durch entsprechende Konjunktionen (Satzverbindungen/Bindewörter wie „and" oder „but") hergestellt werden. In den ersten beiden Übungsaufgaben kannst du dies gezielt trainieren. Versuche dann auch bei den weiteren Schreibaufgaben auf sprachliche Abwechslung bzw. auf die Verknüpfung von Sätzen durch Konjunktionen zu achten.

Arbeitsschritt 5

- Lies deinen Text am Ende noch einmal in Ruhe durch. Ist alles logisch aufgebaut? Gibt es auch keine Gedankensprünge? Wichtig ist auch, dass du alles noch einmal gezielt nach Rechtschreib- und Grammatikfehlern durchsiehst und diese ausbesserst.

Die häufigsten Aufgabenformate in der Prüfung

Folgende Aufgabenformate können in der Abschlussprüfung vorkommen:

Bilder als Schreibanlässe

In der Prüfung können dir Bilder vorgelegt werden, zu denen du eine Geschichte verfassen musst.

- Manchmal wird dir ein Bild als „**visueller Impuls**", d. h. als optischer Schreibanlass vorgegeben. Dann sollst du das Bild als „Aufhänger" für eine kurze Geschichte verwenden. In diesem Fall empfiehlt es sich, das Bild zuerst einmal genau zu betrachten. Eine detaillierte Bildbeschreibung ist allerdings selten nötig, vielmehr sollst du deiner Fantasie freien Lauf lassen.
- Dir können aber auch mehrere Bilder vorgelegt werden, die eine **Bildergeschichte** erzählen. Deine Aufgabe besteht dann z. B. darin, die Geschichte aufzuschreiben, die dir die Bilder erzählen. Es kann auch sein, dass du dir das Ende der Bildergeschichte selbst ausdenken musst.

Formulare und Fragebögen

Das Ausfüllen von Formularen ist ein oft verwendetes Aufgabenformat. Dabei kann es sich z. B. um das Ausfüllen eines Formulars zum Einchecken im Hotel, oder zum Aufnehmen einer Zeugenaussage bei der Polizei, oder um das Ausfüllen von Bewerbungsformularen handeln.

Oft musst du zunächst Angaben zu deiner Person machen (Name, Adresse, Alter usw.) Im Anschluss gilt es meist, Fragen zu bestimmten Themen zu beantworten. Im Hotel wird beispielsweise die Dauer des Aufenthalts erfragt, bei einer Bewerbung ist mit der Frage zu rechnen, warum man sich für den Job interessiert und/oder eignet, bei Zeugenaussagen sind Fragen nach dem beobachteten Tathergang wahrscheinlich. Da der Platz auf einem Formular normalerweise knapp bemessen ist, musst du dich bei diesen Antworten kurz fassen. Oft sind sogar nur Stichpunkte gefragt.

Briefe, E-Mails, Nachrichten und Beiträge in Internetforen

Die Bandbreite an Aufgaben zum Verfassen von eigenen Texten ist groß. Dabei können sowohl formelle als auch persönliche Briefe oder E-Mails verlangt sein, sowie kurze Nachrichten an Freunde oder Beiträge in einem Internetforum. Auf diese Weise wird überprüft, wie gut du in der Lage bist, dich in Alltagssituationen schriftlich auf Englisch auszudrücken.

- **Formelle Texte:** Achte darauf, dass du keine umgangssprachlichen Ausdrücke und Formulierungen verwendest. Vermeide auch Kurzformen wie „I'm". Bleibe in deiner Ausdrucksweise sachlich und nüchtern.
- **Persönliche Texte:** Hier musst du oft einem Freund/einer Freundin schreiben und ihn/sie über bestimmte Geschehnisse informieren. Du kannst deinen Text dabei in einem umgangssprachlicheren Stil verfassen.

Falls dir vorgegeben wird, was deine Mail oder Nachricht enthalten sollte, so achte darauf, auf alle Punkte einzugehen!

TIPP

- Lies die Aufgabenstellung genau durch. Was wird von dir verlangt? Sind Punkte vorgegeben?
- Erstelle eine Stoffsammlung/Mindmap.
- Arbeite deinen Text sorgfältig aus. Versuche dabei, einen gut strukturierten und sprachlich abwechslungsreichen Text zu schreiben.
- Lies abschließend alles noch einmal genau durch und überprüfe dabei, ob alles logisch aufgebaut und verständlich geschrieben ist. Bessere Rechtschreib- und Grammatikfehler aus.

4.2 Hilfreiche Wendungen zur Textproduktion

Anrede und Schlussformeln

Persönlicher Brief/persönliche E-Mail

Liebe Jenny,	Dear Jenny,
Hi/Hallo Jenny,	Hi/Hello Jenny,
Viele Grüße	Best wishes
Liebe Grüße	Love *(nur bei guten Freunden, häufiger von Frauen verwendet als von Männern)*
Mach's gut/Tschüss, Ciao	Take care/Cheers

Formelles Schreiben

wenn du den Namen des Ansprechpartners nicht kennst:

Sehr geehrte Damen und Herren,	Dear Sir or Madam,
Mit freundlichen Grüßen	Yours faithfully

wenn du den Namen des Ansprechpartners kennst:

Sehr geehrter Herr James,	Dear Mr James,
bei einer verheirateten Frau	Dear Mrs Roberts,
bei einer unverheirateten Frau	Dear Miss Berry,
wenn du nicht weißt, ob die Frau verheiratet ist	Dear Ms Bell,
Mit freundlichen Grüßen	Yours sincerely

Einleitung und Schluss eines Briefes/einer E-Mail

Danke für …	Thank you for …
Ich hoffe, dass …	I hope that …
Wie geht es dir/Ihnen?	How are you?
In deiner letzten E-Mail hast du mir über … erzählt.	In your last e-mail you told me about …
In deiner letzten E-Mail hast du mir erzählt, dass …	In your last e-mail you told me that …
Entschuldige, dass ich … vergessen habe, aber …	Sorry that I forgot to …, but …
Sage bitte … / Richte … bitte aus	Please tell …
Es wäre schön, wenn wir uns treffen.	It would be nice if we could meet.
Bitte richte … Grüße aus.	Best wishes to … (Please) say hi/hello to …
Bitte schreibe mir bald zurück.	Write soon.
Ich freue mich darauf, bald von dir zu hören.	I'm looking forward to hearing from you soon.
Ich freue mich auf deine E-Mail.	I'm looking forward to your e-mail.
Ich werde dich anrufen.	I'll call/phone/ring you.

Häufig vorkommende Redewendungen/Ausdrücke

sich entschuldigen	I'm sorry
etwas bedauern	It's a pity/shame that … / I'm disappointed that …
an etwas erinnern	Please remember to …
Überraschung äußern	I was surprised that …
eine Bitte äußern	Could you/Would you …, please?
einen Wunsch äußern	I'd like to …
einen Entschluss mitteilen	I've decided to … I've made up my mind to … I'm going to …
eine Absicht mitteilen	I intend to/I'm planning to … I want to/I will …

eine Meinung äußern	I think that ... I believe that ... I'm of the opinion that ...
Interesse ausdrücken	I'm interested in ...
Freude ausdrücken	I'm happy/glad about ...
Überzeugung ausdrücken	I'm convinced that ... I'm sure that ...
nach dem Preis fragen	How much is it?/ How much does it cost?
Ich hoffe, dir hat ... gefallen.	I hope you liked/enjoyed ...
Ich muss jetzt ...	I have (got) to ...
Ich denke, es ist besser ...	I think it's better to ...

Auskunft geben über sich selbst

Ich wohne in ...	I live in ...
Ich wurde am ... in ... geboren.	I was born in ... on ...
Ich interessiere mich für ...	I'm interested in ...
Ich war schon in ...	I've (already) been to ...
Ich möchte gerne ... werden.	I'd like to be a/an ...
Mir geht es gut.	I'm fine.
Mir geht es nicht gut.	I'm not well.
Ich mag ... *Ich mag ... lieber (als ...).*	I like ... / I enjoy ... I prefer to ... / I like ... better (than ...)
Ich weiß ... noch nicht genau.	I still don't know exactly.
Ich plane, (etwas zu tun).	I plan to ...
Ich freue mich (sehr) auf ...	I'm looking forward to ... I'm excited about ...
Ich konnte ... nicht ...	I wasn't able to ... / I couldn't ...
In meiner Freizeit	In my free time/spare time
Ich nehme (regelmäßig) an ... teil.	I take part in ...

Layout eines formellen englischen Briefs

24 Castle Street Blackburn Lancashire LK6 5TQ	Absender (ohne Namen)[1]
6 March 20...	Datum[2]
Mrs J. Fox Dane Cleaners 3 Arthur Road Doddington NE3 6LD	Empfänger (nur in förmlichen Briefen)
Dear Mrs Fox,	Anrede
Thank you for your letter ...	Brief
Yours sincerely,	Schlussformel
Adam Smith	Unterschrift
Adam Smith	Name

1 Die Adresse des Absenders kann auch auf der linken Seite stehen

2 *Auch möglich: 6th March 20... oder March 6, 20...; das Datum kann auch links stehen*

4.3 Übungsaufgaben zum Kompetenzbereich „Writing“

Sprachliche Ausdrucksfähigkeit

1. Fill in the correct conjunctions:

when • while • in order to • because • but

a) I took an umbrella with me this morning ____________________ it was raining.

b) ____________ I'm 18 years old I will leave home.

c) I'd love to visit New York, ____________ I don't have enough money.

d) Jack moved to another town ____________________ become independent.

e) Clara washes the dishes ________________ she's talking to her best friend on the phone.

2. Fill in an appropriate expression *(einen passenden Ausdruck)* from the following list to complete the text.

but • In my opinion • and • Secondly • but all in all I believe that • Another aspect is that • First of all • In addition to that • you could argue that

Hi, my name is Amy, I am 16 years old and I love watching talent shows such as "The Voice". ________________________________, talent shows are great. ______________________, they give people the chance to show their musical talent to a big audience. ______________________, these shows can also give them the chance to earn money with their music. ______________________ some young people are not very self-confident, ________________ when they are given the opportunity to be on stage and to get applause, their self-confidence can grow.

______________________________, people who make it to the finals get a lot of tips about how to find their own style. Of course, ____________________________________ the fame and the money don't make anyone happy ________________ that these shows are too much stress for young people, ____ talent shows help the participants to develop their musical talents.

Visuelle Impulse (Bilder und Bildergeschichten)

3. Look at the picture and do the tasks.

a) Describe what you see on the left-hand side and in the background.

b) Describe what you see on the right-hand side of the picture.

c) Imagine where the couple would like to go and why they would want to go there.

4. Use these pictures to write a story in English for a competition. Don't forget to write a headline and an ending, too. Write 60–80 words.

Eine Geschichte zu Ende erzählen

5. Read the beginning of the story and finish it.

   I was on my way to a friend's house.
   While I was walking through the park I saw …

   Write about **60 words**.

   Include the following ideas:
   - What did you see in the park?
   - What did you do?
   - How does it end?

6. Read the beginning of the story and finish it.

   Last summer I went to Italy with my family.
   In Rome …

   Write about **80 words**.

   Include the following ideas:
   - What did you want to do?
   - Was there an unexpected event?
   - How does it end?

Formulare

7. Your student magazine is doing a survey among the pupils at your school. Fill in the form below.

What year are you in?	☐ 5 ☐ 6 ☐ 7 ☐ 8 ☐ 9 ☐ 10
How do you get to school?	
How long does it take you to get to school?	
What is your favourite subject?	
What do you like about our school? Name two things.	• ______ • ______
What do you not like about our school? Name two things.	• ______ • ______
What do you think about the technical equipment?	
What do you think about the sports facilities (gym, sports field)?	

8. You have finished school and you are going on a four-week Interrail trip through Europe. At the travel agency you are asked to fill in the following form:

INTERRAIL GLOBAL PASS

valid for travel in 30 European countries

Ticket Details

LAST NAME:	FIRST NAME:
DATE OF BIRTH: Day ________	Month ________ Year ________
SEX:	NATIONALITY:
HOME ADDRESS: Street: ____________ Zip Code: ________ Town: ____________ Country: ____________	
TYPE of TICKET:	☐ youth ☐ adult
STARTING DATE:	
END OF TRIP:	
HOW DID YOU FIND OUT ABOUT THE INTERRAIL GLOBAL PASS?	

9. Your first destination is Greece. In Athens you meet someone from the National Tourist Board, who tells you that if you fill in the questionnaire on Greece, you can win a one-week holiday for two in a luxury hotel not far from Athens. Of course you fill in the form:

FULL NAME:	
HOME ADDRESS:	
E-MAIL:	
AGE:	
SEX:	NATIONALITY:
How did you get to Greece?	
Where are you staying?	
How long are you staying in Greece?	
What do you like best about Greece?	
Could you also imagine travelling to Greece in winter? Why? / Why not?	

THANK YOU FOR TAKING PART IN OUR SURVEY!

E-Mails, Briefe, Nachrichten und Beiträge in Internetforen

10. What is the correct start and ending for a letter or an e-mail? You are writing to:

a) your aunt Mary:

____

b) Mrs Smith at the bank:

____

c) your friend Luke:

____

d) Mr O'Brien, your English teacher:

____

e) a postcard to your grandparents:

____

f) the addressee of your job application (you do not know his/her name):

____

11. You read a post in a music forum on the internet. It says that musicals are boring and old-fashioned. Below, you find your response to the post. Use the questions to complete the text. Write about **60** words.

Dear Jack,

I read your post about musicals.
(Agree or disagree with the post.)

____

(Have you ever been to a musical? Write something about it: where it was, how you liked it.)

____

____

____

(Do you recommend that people go and see a musical?)

____

____

Kind regards,
(your name)

12. You went to Hamburg to see the musical "Lion King" and you send this picture to your English friend Kim, who wants to know more about the musical and your stay in Hamburg.

Great picture, huh?
Greetings from Hamburg where I went to see "The Lion King"!

Kim: Wow! How was the show?

You: ______________________________

____

Kim: Was it expensive?

You: ______________________________

____

Kim: Who did you go with?

You: ______________________________

____

Kim: Where are you staying?

You: ______________________________

____

Kim: How did you get to Hamburg?

You: ______________________________

____

Kim: What is Hamburg like and what have you already seen of the city?

You: ______________________________

____

Kim: When are you back? Maybe we could meet sometime soon!

You: ______________________________

____

13. You want to earn some extra money in your summer holidays and improve your English. You have seen this advert:

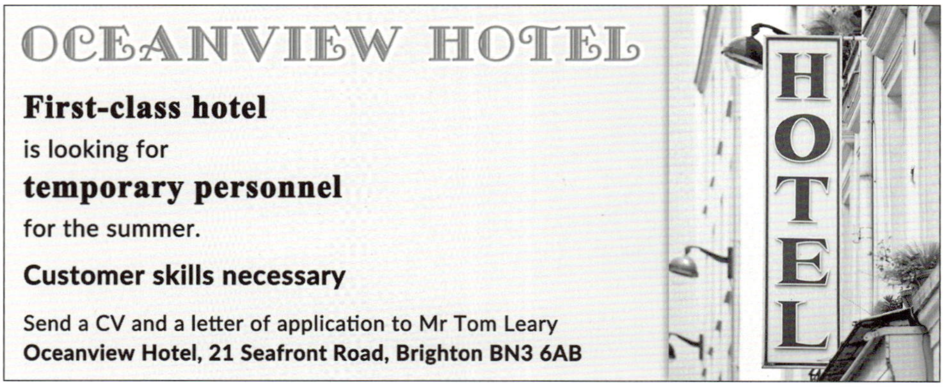

Complete the letter of application. Write about **60** words.

Write about …
- yourself.
- why are you interested in the job.
- why you are qualified for the job.

Here are some things you might want to ask for:
- working hours
- salary *(Gehalt)*

______________________________,

I am interested in working at Oceanview Hotel in the summer.

____

____

____

____

____

____

____

____

____

____

____

I am looking forward to hearing from you.

Yours ______________________________,
(your name)

14. Your English friend Jason asked you about your holiday plans. Write him a message of about **80** words.

Tell him …
- where you are going on holiday.
- when you are going.
- who is going with you.
- what you are planning to do.

15. Your aunt Sarah lives in England. You are staying with her in the summer holidays. As you would like to earn some money and improve your English you apply for the following job. Write about **80** words.

Write about …
- yourself.
- your qualifications.
- why you would be suited for the job.

16. On an Internet forum you find the following discussion: "Should teenagers be allowed to vote at the age of 16?"
Write about ...
- pros.
- cons.
- your own opinion.

Write a post of about **80** words.

5 Kompetenzbereich: Speaking

Immer wieder wird im Unterricht deine mündliche Kommunikationsfähigkeit überprüft. Auch im Rahmen der Hauptschulabschlussprüfung gibt es einen mündlichen Prüfungsteil. Das so genannte „oral exam" findet ein paar Wochen vor der schriftlichen Prüfung statt; die mündliche Note fließt mit einem Drittel in das Gesamtergebnis der Abschlussprüfung ein.

5.1 Strategien zum Kompetenzbereich „Speaking"

Langfristige Vorbereitung

Sich in einer Fremdsprache mündlich auszudrücken, ist nicht einfach. Man kann sich auch nicht kurzfristig – sozusagen über Nacht – auf diesen Prüfungsbereich vorbereiten. Will man in einer mündlichen Prüfung gut abschneiden, dann muss man **langfristig** und **nachhaltig** an der Sprechfertigkeit arbeiten.
Übungsmöglichkeiten bietet dir dein Englischunterricht. Nimm aktiv am Unterricht teil, d. h., melde dich so oft wie möglich und sprich auf Englisch. So gewinnst du mit der Zeit Routine und wirst gelassener. Wenn du dabei noch die folgenden grundsätzlichen Tipps und Hinweise berücksichtigst, klappt das Sprechen mit der Zeit sicherlich recht gut.

TIPP

- Nutze die Übungsphasen im Unterricht.
- Sprich deutlich und nicht zu schnell.
- Frage nach, wenn du etwas nicht verstanden hast.
- Vermeide einfache, kurze Antworten wie „yes" oder „no". Mit solchen Antworten kannst du keine Gespräche in Gang halten und auch deine mündliche Ausdrucksfähigkeit nicht unter Beweis stellen. Wenn es passend ist, begründe deine Meinung oder füge ein Beispiel an.
- Wenn du unsicher oder nervös bist, bilde lieber kürzere Sätze.
- Lerne die hilfreichen Wendungen (siehe 5.3) auswendig und baue sie immer wieder in deine Sätze ein. Auf diese Weise werden sie Teil deines aktiven Wortschatzes und es wird dir leicht fallen, sie auch in der mündlichen Prüfung zu verwenden.
- Bemühe dich, Sachverhalte auf unterschiedliche Weise auszudrücken, um zu zeigen, dass du einen vielfältigen Wortschatz hast. Beschränke dich also z. B. nicht auf „I think", um deine Meinung auszudrücken.
- Versuche, dich auch in deiner Freizeit mit der englischen Sprache zu beschäftigen. Du kannst z. B. englische Zeitschriften oder Bücher lesen, Fernsehsendungen oder Filme auf Englisch ansehen, ein Tagebuch auf Englisch führen oder die Grundeinstellung deines Handys auf die Fremdsprache ändern. Auf diese Weise wirst du immer vertrauter und sicherer im Gebrauch des Englischen.

5.2 Das „oral exam" der Hauptschulabschlussprüfung

Ablauf der Prüfung

- Es werden meist zwei Schüler gleichzeitig geprüft – in Ausnahmefällen auch drei. Wer mit wem zusammen geprüft wird, wird einige Tage vor der Prüfung per Los entschieden. Du brauchst aber keine Angst zu haben, denn auch wenn dein Partner nicht so gut in Englisch ist, kannst du trotzdem die volle Punktzahl bekommen, da jeder Schüler gesondert bewertet wird.
- Es sind immer zwei Lehrer dabei. In der Regel sind das dein Englischlehrer bzw. deine Englischlehrerin und noch ein zweiter Fachlehrer. Dein Lehrer führt das Prüfungsgespräch mit dir und deinem Mitschüler, der andere Lehrer sitzt dabei, hört genau zu und schreibt das Protokoll.
- Das „oral exam" dauert etwa 12–15 Minuten.

Prüfungsteile

Das „oral exam" besteht aus zwei (G-Kurs) bzw. drei Teilen (E-Kurs) mit jeweils verschiedenen Aufgabenstellungen. Zwar sind die Bestandteile der Prüfung vom Ministerium festgelegt, die genaue Ausarbeitung der Prüfung findet aber an deiner Schule statt. Höre deinem Lehrer also genau zu, wenn er euch wichtige Informationen zur Prüfung gibt.

Part I

- **Warm-up / Speaking about yourself**
  Nach einer kurzen Begrüßung und Vorstellung des Zweitprüfers erkundigt sich dein Lehrer, wie es dir geht. Danach stellt er dir Fragen, bei denen du etwas über dich selbst bzw. deine Lebensumstände erzählen sollst. Es kann sein, dass du z. B. auch deinen Namen oder deine Straße buchstabieren musst. Wiederhole also unbedingt noch einmal das „spelling alphabet".
  Die Fragen können im Allgemeinen vier Bereichen zugeordnet werden:
  – *my family*
  – *my city/town/village*
  – *my hobbies/my free-time activities*
  – *my school/my class/my course/my career*

TIPP

Auf diesen Teil kannst du dich schon lange vor der Prüfung vorbereiten, indem du dir Aussagen zu deiner Familie, deinem Wohnort, deinen Hobbys etc. überlegst. Bereite z. B. „mind maps" vor, in denen du verschiedene Aspekte notierst. Du kannst sie im Laufe der Zeit immer wieder ergänzen. Übe regelmäßig, und am besten mit jemandem, der dir Rückmeldung geben und dich verbessern kann. Dadurch, dass du dir nur Stichpunkte notierst, bleibst du sprachlich flexibler und kannst in der mündlichen Prüfung besser auf die Fragen deines Lehrers reagieren.

Part II

Information gap activity

Hier wird dir und deinem Mitschüler eine bestimmte Situation anhand von Stichpunkten vorgestellt, in die ihr euch hineinversetzen müsst. Ihr müsst euch nun miteinander unterhalten und gemäß euren Rollenvorgaben Informationen austauschen. Wichtig ist, dass ihr jeweils auf die Äußerungen des anderen eingeht, sodass ein echter Dialog entsteht. Rückfragen an den Gesprächspartner eignen sich hierfür auch sehr gut. Im Gespräch soll aufeinander eingegangen und nicht einfach etwas gesagt werden, das nicht zum Redebeitrag des anderen passt.

TIPP

- Übe immer wieder mit verschiedenen Mitschülern.
- Sieh dir das ausgehändigte Material in Ruhe an und nimm dir die Zeit, die Vorgaben genau durchzulesen.
- Höre deinem Gesprächspartner aufmerksam zu. Wenn du seine Aussage oder Frage nicht verstanden hast, traue dich, nachzufragen. Nur so kannst du angemessen auf den Redebeitrag deines Partners reagieren.

Part III

Speaking prompts (nur Kurs E)

Hier musst du ein Bild bzw. Foto beschreiben und näher untersuchen. Abschließend ist es deine Aufgabe, die dargestellte Situation auf dich selbst zu beziehen und z. B. über deine Vorlieben für und Abneigungen gegen die abgebildete Aktivität oder Gegebenheit (wie z. B. eine bestimmte Sportart) zu sprechen. Du kannst alles sagen, was dir zu deinem Bild einfällt. Wichtig ist, dass du englisch sprichst. Kleinere Grammatikfehler sind nicht so gravierend. Du kannst trotz einiger Fehler immer noch die volle Punktzahl erhalten. Entscheidend ist, dass der Inhalt deiner Äußerungen verständlich ist. Du hast ca. zwei Minuten Zeit, um über das Bild sprechen. Danach können sich Fragen deines Lehrers anschließen, die du beantworten sollst.

TIPP

Sieh dir das Foto genau an und beschreibe es im Detail. Nutze die dir zur Verfügung stehende Zeit und sage alles, was dir zu dem Bild einfällt. Gerate nicht in Panik, wenn dir ein wichtiges Wort fehlt. Konzentriere dich bei deiner Beschreibung dann einfach auf andere Aspekte.

Folgende Fragen können dir dabei helfen, deine Antwort zu strukturieren:

- *What is happening?*
- *How many people are in the picture? How old are they? Where are they? What do they look like? What are they wearing? What is their relationship to each other?*
- *When or where was the photo taken? Why are these people in this place?*
- *What is the main theme or message?*
- *What else can you say about it?*
- *What do you think about the picture? Why do/don't you like it? …*

5.3 Hilfreiche Wendungen zum „oral exam“

Bildbeschreibung *(Describing pictures)*

In the picture I / we can see …	*In dem Bild kann ich/können wir … sehen.*
The photo shows …	*Das Foto zeigt …*
It was taken in …	*Es wurde in … aufgenommen.*
In the background / foreground there is / there are …	*Im Hintergrund/Vordergrund ist/ sind …*
In the centre / middle of the picture …	*In der Bildmitte …*
On the left / right of the photo …	*Links/Rechts auf dem Foto …*
The person in the top left-hand / bottom right-hand corner …	*Die Person in der linken oberen/ rechten unteren Ecke …*
At the top/ bottom you can see …	*Oben/Unten kann man … sehen.*
Next to / Near …	*Neben/In der Nähe …*
Behind / In front of …	*Hinter/Vor …*
On top of / Under …	*Auf/Unter …*
Between … and …	*Zwischen … und …*

Mit folgenden Ausdrücken kannst du Vermutungen anstellen und deine Meinung über das Bild ausdrücken:

It seems as if …	*Es scheint, als ob …*
The boy seems to …	*Der Junge scheint zu …*
Maybe/Perhaps …	*Vielleicht …*
The atmosphere is happy / sad / …	*Die Stimmung ist fröhlich/traurig …*
I (don't) like the photo, because …	*Ich mag das Foto (nicht), weil …*
The photo makes me think of/ reminds me of …	*Das Foto erinnert mich an …*

Eine eigene Meinung ausdrücken *(Expressing an opinion)*

I (don't) think / believe / expect / imagine / suppose (that) …	*Ich glaube (nicht), (dass) …*
In my opinion / view …	*Meiner Meinung nach …*
That's not my opinion.	*Das ist nicht meine Meinung.*
I'm (not) sure/certain …	*Ich bin (nicht) sicher …*
I (don't) doubt (that) …	*Ich bezweifle (nicht), dass …*
I would / wouldn't …	*Ich würde (nicht) …*
I would like / I'd like …	*Ich würde/möchte gern …*
I don't like / I dislike …	*Ich mag … nicht.*
I would / wouldn't prefer …	*Ich würde lieber (nicht) …*

I'm for ...	*Ich bin für ... / dafür, dass ...*
I'm against ...	*Ich bin gegen ... / dagegen, dass ...*

Andere nach ihrer Meinung fragen *(Asking other people for their opinion)*

What do you think about ...?	*Was denkst du über ...?*
What's your opinion on / view on / reaction to ...?	*Was ist deine Meinung zu ...? / Was denkst du über ...?*
How do you see/view this/ the situation?	*Wie siehst du das/die Situation?*
What would you say about ...?	*Was würdest du über / zum Thema ... sagen?*
How do you (personally) feel about ...?	*Was hältst du (persönlich) von ...?*
Could you explain something to me?	*Könntest du mir etwas erklären?*
What about (the prohibition of drinking alcohol in public places)? Do you think that's right?	*Was denkst du über (das Verbot, Alkohol in der Öffentlichkeit zu trinken)? Glaubst du, dass das richtig / in Ordnung ist?*
I don't suppose you'll / you would agree, will you / would you? *(eine Antwort fordernd)*	*Du wirst sicher nicht zustimmen, oder?*

Du kannst auch Fragen mit Verneinungen stellen, um deinen Gesprächspartner zu einer Meinungsäußerung zu bringen:

Don't you think that ...?	*Glaubst du nicht, dass ...?*
Wouldn't you like to see ...?	*Hättest du nicht auch lieber ...?*
Shouldn't we ...?	*Sollten wir nicht ...?*

Zustimmen und widersprechen *(Agreeing and disagreeing)*

This is / That's true.	*Das stimmt.*
I agree (with you).	*Ich bin deiner Meinung.*
(I'm sorry but) I disagree (with you).	*Ich bin nicht deiner Meinung.*
Yes, of course.	*Ja, natürlich.*
No, not at all.	*Nein, ganz und gar nicht.*
That's a good / great / fantastic idea.	*Das ist ein guter / großartiger / fantastischer Vorschlag.*
Excuse me but I think that's a bad idea / That's a bad idea.	*Das ist kein guter Gedanke / keine gute Idee.*
You're right (about/that ...)	*Du hast Recht (mit / wenn du sagst, dass ...).*
I'm sorry, but you're wrong (about ... / about that).	*Das stimmt nicht.*

Wenn du entsprechende Adverbien vor „right“, „wrong“ und „understand“ stellst, gibst du deiner Antwort noch mehr Nachdruck.

You're absolutely right.	*Du hast völlig recht.*
You're totally wrong.	*Du liegst völlig falsch.*
I think you don't really understand (the problem).	*Ich glaube, du verstehst (das Problem) überhaupt nicht.*

Wenn du dir mit deiner Meinung nicht sicher bist, verwende Ausdrücke wie:

I'm not sure/certain.	*Ich bin (mir) nicht sicher.*

Jemanden unterbrechen *(Interrupting someone)*

Can I ask you something?	*Kann ich dich etwas fragen?*
Can/May I (just) say something, please?	*Kann ich bitte etwas sagen?*
Excuse me, but …	*Entschuldigung, aber …*
I don't wish/I'm sorry to interrupt/stop you but …	*Ich möchte dich nicht unterbrechen, aber …/Ich unterbreche dich ungern, aber …*
I'm sorry, I don't agree with …	*Ich bin anderer Meinung (als) …*
I'm sorry, that's not right/fair.	*Das ist nicht richtig/fair.*
I'm sorry, but (I'd just like to say) …	*Es tut mir leid, aber …*
You're wrong there. *(nachdrücklich)*	*Du hast nicht Recht./Da hast du mit Sicherheit nicht Recht.*
I don't think you're right.	*Ich glaube, dass du nicht Recht hast.*
Oh, come on! You don't really believe that.	*Das glaubst du doch selbst nicht.*
How can you say that?	*Wie kannst du das sagen?*

Darum bitten, dass etwas wiederholt wird.
(Asking for something to be repeated)

Excuse me, could you say that again, please?	*Kannst du das bitte noch einmal sagen?*
Sorry, could you repeat that/what you said about …?	*Kannst du das bitte wiederholen?/… bitte wiederholen, was du über…* gesagt hast?
I'm sorry/I'm afraid I didn't quite hear/catch/understand what you said. Could you say it again/repeat it, please?	*Es tut mir leid, aber ich habe nicht genau verstanden, was du meinst/gesagt hast. Kannst du das bitte noch einmal sagen?*
I'm sorry/I'm afraid, I missed/forgot what you were saying (about …).	*Es tut mir leid, ich habe nicht verstanden, was du (über …) gesagt*

Could you explain it again / once more, please?	*hast. Kannst du mir das noch einmal erklären?*
I'm sorry / I'm afraid, you were talking a bit too fast for me – could you say it again a little bit more slowly / would you mind repeating what you said, please?	*Es tut mir leid, du hast für mich etwas zu schnell gesprochen. Könntest du das bitte etwas langsamer wiederholen?/Es tut mir leid, das war ein wenig zu schnell für mich. Könntest du es bitte etwas langsamer wiederholen?*

Ein bereits behandeltes Thema aufgreifen *(Returning to an earlier topic)*

You said earlier …	*Du hast vorhin gesagt …*
You mentioned / talked about …	*Du hast … erwähnt.*
A few minutes ago you said …	*Vor ein paar Minuten hast du gesagt …*
As you said before …	*Wie du vorhin/schon gesagt hast, …*
Can we go back to … for a minute?	*Können wir noch einmal auf … zurückkommen?*

Das Thema wechseln *(Changing the subject)*

We've talked a lot about … Could we look at … now?	*Wir haben viel über … geredet. Könnten wir jetzt über … sprechen?*
Can we move on and talk about …?	*Können wir weitermachen und über … reden?*
We should really talk about … too.	*Wir sollten wirklich auch über … reden.*
That's my opinion about (tennis). But what about (football)? What do you think about it?	*So denke ich über (Tennis). Aber was meinst du zu (Fußball)?*
Can we talk about … now?	*Können wir jetzt über … sprechen?*
Perhaps we should also talk about …	*Vielleicht sollten wir auch über … reden.*
Can / May I say something at this point?	*Kann ich an dieser Stelle etwas sagen?*

Andere zum Reden bringen *(Making people talk)*

Zum Beispiel direkte Fragen mit Fragewörtern: „what", „why", „where", „when", „who", „which", „how"

What do you think, (Anne)?	*Was meinst du, (Anne)?*
Why do / don't you think so?	*Warum glaubst du das (nicht)?*
Can we find a solution together?	*Können wir zusammen eine Lösung finden?*

Entscheidungsfragen

Are you interested in …?	*Interessierst du dich für …?*
Do you want …?	*Willst du …?*

Bestätigungsfragen

The weather is terrible, isn't it?	*Das Wetter ist scheußlich, oder?*
It isn't cold outside, is it?	*Es ist nicht kalt draußen, oder?*

TIPP

Manchmal musst du kurz überlegen, bis du weißt, was du sagen möchtest. Damit das Gespräch dennoch nicht unterbrochen wird, kannst du folgende Füllwörter benutzen:

- *Well, …*
- *Let me see … / I see …*
- *I'm not sure, but …*
- *What I'm trying to say is …*
- *Actually, I think …*
- *I guess …*

Lerne diese Ausdrücke auswendig und versuche, sie bereits während des Unterrichts im Gespräch anzuwenden.

Wenn einer von euch nicht mehr weiter weiß, kann der andere mit solchen Fragen helfen:

- *Are you saying that …?*
- *What do you think about …? / Don't you think that …?*

5.4 Übungsaufgaben zum Kompetenzbereich „Speaking"

Oral exam – Part I

Hinweis

In diesem Teil musst du etwas über dich selbst erzählen. In der folgenden Übung sollst du in Vorbereitung auf ein mögliches Prüfungsthema eine „mind map" erstellen.

1. Make a mind map of your family. The following aspects might help you. Feel free to add other details, too.
   - your family members' names
   - their ages
   - your parents' jobs
   - your family members' hobbies
   - your house/your flat
   - the activities you do together
   - where you have gone on holiday/are planning to go on holiday
   - what you like / don't like about your family
   - your grandparents / aunts / uncles …
   - your pet
   - …

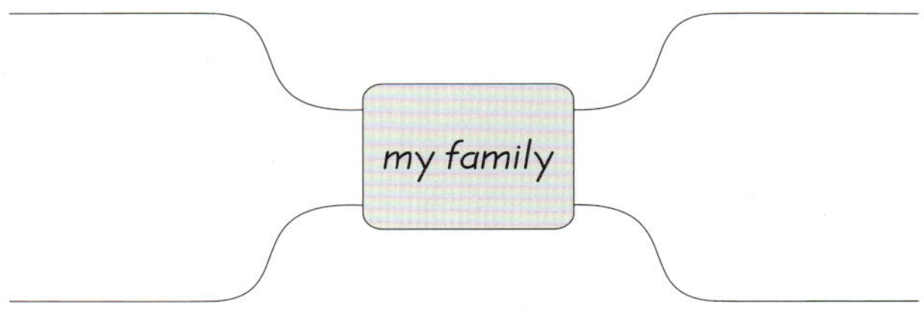

Hinweis

In einem zweiten Schritt übst du deine Präsentation, indem du versuchst, mithilfe deiner „mind map" eine zusammenhängende und gut strukturierte Antwort auf die Frage deines Lehrers zu geben.

2. TEACHER: Tell me something about your family.
   YOU: Well, in my family, there are …

Oral exam – Part II: Information gap activity

Hinweis

Im zweiten Teil der mündlichen Prüfung führst du mit deinem Mitschüler/deiner Mitschülerin ein Gespräch zu einem vorgegebenen Thema. Es kann sein, dass ihr Rollenkarten bekommt, die unterschiedliche Informationen enthalten. Die Stichpunkte auf euren Rollenkarten führen euch als roter Faden durch das Gespräch. Dabei kann es sich z. B. um ein Verkaufsgespräch im Supermarkt oder an der Kinokasse, um ein Gespräch mit einem Austauschschüler oder um die Organisation einer Party/Schulveranstaltung handeln (Aufgabe 3).

3. "At the cinema"

Teacher: In this part of the test you are going to talk to each other. One of you wants to buy cinema tickets, the other one works at the ticket office. When you have read your prompts, you can start with your dialogue.

Rollenkarte A

You are on a trip through Great Britain and want to go to a cinema. You go to the ticket office to buy tickets for yourself and two of your friends. It is now 6.30 p.m.

Here are some prompts you can use:

- tickets for "The Royal Family"?
- number of tickets: 3
- time film ends?
- where to buy popcorn, something to drink?

Rollenkarte B

You sell tickets at the cinema in Birmingham. You are talking to the customer. It is now 6.30 p.m.

Here are some prompts you can use:

- how many tickets?
- £ 6 back rows, £ 4 front rows
- student ID? Ticket £ 1 cheaper
- end: 9.30 p.m.
- interested in film poster? → cinema shop

Oral exam – Part III: Speaking prompts (nur Kurs E)

Hinweis

Im letzten Prüfungsteil legt man dir und deinem Mitschüler jeweils ein Bild vor. Du musst zunächst im Detail beschreiben, was du auf dem Bild siehst, und dann ein paar persönliche Gedanken äußern. Du hast ca. zwei Minuten Zeit, alles über das Bild zu sagen, was dir einfällt. Wenn du ins Stocken gerätst, wird dir dein Lehrer Fragen stellen, die dir helfen, deine Redezeit zu nutzen.

4. **Teacher** (to Candidate A): Describe the picture, please.

Hinweis

Die Fragen deines Lehrers, die sich an deine Bildbeschreibung anschließen können, hängen natürlich davon ab, auf welche Aspekte du bereits eingegangen bist. Mögliche „prompts" (Hilfestellungen) könnten z. B. sein:

Teacher:
- What has happened?/What will happen next?
- What could be the problem?
- Why are they sitting at the computer?

5. **Teacher** (to Candidate B): Describe the picture, please.

Possible prompts:

Teacher:
- What could the children be talking about?
- How is the girl feeling?
- What could happen next?
- Do you know anyone who has been in a situation like this?

Original-Prüfungsaufgaben

Hauptschulabschlussprüfung Niedersachsen
Englisch 2020

Kurse E und G

I. Listening

Part 1: Questions 1–6

Worksheet
6 Punkte

You will hear six short conversations.
You will hear each conversation twice.
For each question there are three pictures and a short recording.
Choose the correct picture and put a tick (✓) in the box below it.

Example:

0. Which tickets do they buy?

A ☐

B ☐

C ☑

1. When does the drama group meet?

A ☐

B ☐

C ☐

2. Who is going to do the dishes?

A ☐

B ☐

C ☐

3. Which room does the guest get?

A ☐

B ☐

C ☐

4. How does Kevin get to his job interview?

A ☐

B ☐

C ☐

5. Where do the tourists go first?

A ☐

B ☐

C ☐

6. What's the weather like today?

A ☐

B ☐

C ☐

Kurs E

Part 2: Questions 7–12

Job interview

Listen to the following conversation between Kevin and Sandy. Kevin is applying for a job at Sandy's fashion store. 6 Punkte
For questions 7–12 tick (✓) the correct box A, B or C.
The first question is an example.

Example:

0. The applicant's name is …
   - A Sandy Burns. ☐
   - B Kevin Grant. ☑
   - C Kevin Burns. ☐

7. Kevin learned about the job offer …
   - A on the Internet. ☐
   - B at a job fair. ☐
   - C from a friend. ☐

8. One of Kevin's weaknesses is his …
   - A perfectionism. ☐
   - B shyness. ☐
   - C honesty. ☐

9. He says that a job applicant could wear …
   - A jeans. ☐
   - B trainers. ☐
   - C a T-shirt. ☐

10. In Costa Rica, Kevin …
    - A sold coffee. ☐
    - B guided tourists. ☐
    - C worked in a national park. ☐

11. Kevin's best language is …
    - A Spanish. ☐
    - B French. ☐
    - C Polish. ☐

12. At first, Kevin's pay would be …
    - A six pounds per hour. ☐
    - B eight pounds per hour. ☐
    - C ten pounds per hour. ☐

Kurs G

Part 2: Questions 7–12

Job interview

6 Punkte

Listen to the following conversation between Kevin and Sandy. Kevin is applying for a job at Sandy's fashion store.
For questions 7–12 tick (✓) the correct box A, B or C.
The first question is an example.

Example:

0. The applicant's name is …
   - A Sandy Burns. ☐
   - B Kevin Grant. ☑
   - C Kevin Burns. ☐

7. Kevin learned about the job offer …
   - A on the Internet. ☐
   - B at a job fair. ☐
   - C from a friend. ☐

8. One of Kevin's weaknesses is his …
   - A perfectionism. ☐
   - B shyness. ☐
   - C honesty. ☐

9. He says that for a job interview a person could wear …
   - A jeans. ☐
   - B trainers. ☐
   - C a T-shirt. ☐

10. In Costa Rica, Kevin …
    - A sold coffee. ☐
    - B guided tourists. ☐
    - C worked in a national park. ☐

11. Kevin speaks …
    - A Spanish best. ☐
    - B French best. ☐
    - C Polish best. ☐

12. At first, Kevin would get …
    - A six pounds per hour. ☐
    - B eight pounds per hour. ☐
    - C ten pounds per hour. ☐

Kurs E

Part 3: Questions 13–18: Writing competition

Out of Doors Club

Listen to this radio ad for a writing competition.
For questions 13–18 fill in the gaps to complete the notes.
The first question is an example.

6 Punkte

0	Organiser:	*Out of Doors Club*
13	Write about:	______________
14	Number of words:	______________
15	Open to children aged:	______________
16	Prize:	______________
17	Send entries to:	________ @ ______________
18	Entry deadline:	______________

Kurs G

Part 3: Questions 13–18: Writing competition

Out of Doors Club

Listen to this radio ad for a writing competition.
For questions 13–18 fill in the gaps to complete the notes.
The first question is an example.

6 Punkte

0	Organiser:	*Out of Doors Club*
13	Write about:	Your favourite British ______________
14	Number of words:	______________
15	Open to children aged:	9 – ______________
16	Prize:	Free family trip to an ______________
17	Send entries to:	________ @ ______________
18	Entry deadline:	______________

Kurs E

Part 4: Questions 19–25

Interview with a polyglot

7 Punkte *You will hear an interview with Leyla Skovekolá. She talks about different ways of learning a language.*
For questions 19–25 decide whether each sentence is true or false.
Put a tick (✓) in the correct box 'true' or 'false'.
The first question is an example.

		true	false
0.	A polyglot can speak more than one language.	☑	☐
19.	Ms Skovekolá learned to speak English at school.	☐	☐
20.	She developed her own way to learn languages.	☐	☐
21.	She gave up reading Harry Potter because it was too difficult.	☐	☐
22.	Reading her favourite book was a good way to improve her English.	☐	☐
23.	Learning lists of vocabulary is a good way to keep words in your memory.	☐	☐
24.	Talking to yourself does not help you learn languages.	☐	☐
25.	It's difficult to find the time to learn a language.	☐	☐

Kurs G

Part 4: Questions 19–25

Interview with a polyglot

7 Punkte *You will hear an interview with Leyla Skovekolá. She talks about different ways of learning a language.*
For questions 19–25 decide whether each sentence is true or false.
Put a tick (✓) in the correct box 'true' or 'false'.
The first question is an example.

		true	false
0.	A polyglot can speak more than one language.	☑	☐
19.	Ms Skovekolá learned to speak English at school.	☐	☐
20.	She has her own way to learn languages.	☐	☐
21.	She gave up reading Harry Potter because it was too hard.	☐	☐
22.	Reading her favourite book was a good way to learn better English.	☐	☐
23.	Memorizing word lists is a good way to remember words for a long time.	☐	☐
24.	Talking to yourself does not help you with learning languages.	☐	☐
25.	It's hard to find the time to learn a language.	☐	☐

Kurs E

II. Reading

Part 1: Questions 1–5

5 Punkte

Read the texts below. Then read the statements (1–5).
Decide whether the statements are **true** or **false**. Then tick (✓) the correct box.

1.

To rent:
Incredible modern flat on the 2nd floor in London SW 6!

- 2 spacious bedrooms – not furnished
- floor to ceiling windows
- large open kitchen
- 2 minutes from tube station
- Shops and restaurants within walking distance
- £ 850 a month
- Viewing anytime that suits you

Phone 020 933 9458

2.

We buy your phone!

Got a new smartphone? Great!

Why not sell your old one?
We buy all brands and models.

BEST PRICES PAID!

For more information visit our webpage:
www.webuyyourphone.com

3.

4.

Teen Writing Club

For kids in grades 6–10

September 18th – December 18th
(no class Nov 6th)

Tuesdays 4 pm – 5 pm,

Do you like to write and want to share your stories, poems or thoughts?

Join us every Tuesday this autumn at the Spencer Library.
Let's put some great words to paper!

For more information email to
inspiration@spencer-library.com

Spencer Library, 244 East Street, New York

		true	false
1.	The people from *webuyyourphone.com* are interested in new phones.	☐	☐
2.	The two-bedroom flat is only two minutes from shops and restaurants.	☐	☐
3.	The Rhema Theatre Company puts a show together in less than a week.	☐	☐
4.	The teen writing club takes place every Tuesday during the summer.	☐	☐
5.	Young writers can't write poems at the library on the 6th November.	☐	☐

Part 2: Questions 6–10

Edinburgh Castle

5 Punkte

Read these short texts about Edinburgh Castle and decide which headline (A–G) fits each text (6–10) best.
Write the correct letters behind the numbers.

A	A lot to see
B	Used by the army
C	Home to royalty
D	Ancient traditions live on
E	Treat yourself
F	A national symbol
G	Get a tattoo

6. ☐ Edinburgh Castle, situated high above the city on Castle Rock, was once the home of the kings and queens of Scotland. The 700-year-old Crown of Scotland can still be seen there, and the Royal apartments include a small room where James I, who later became King of England, was born in 1566.

7. ☐ Many battles with the English took place at the castle. It was attacked many times over the centuries but was never destroyed. That is why many Scots see it as a symbol of their own survival.

8. ☐ Visitors to the Castle will see a military guard at the gate, because the castle is still the headquarters of the Scottish part of the army. The famous Military Tattoo is also held here every August. This is a spectacular three-week festival of bagpipe and band music.

9. ☐ In Edinburgh Castle you can see exhibitions of Scottish history and a collection of armour and weapons. In addition to what there is to see inside, the castle's hilltop position offers the best views of the city.

10. ☐ The traditional afternoon teas can be one of the great pleasures of a visit to the castle. Enjoy sandwiches, scones, home-baked cake and whole leaf tea. Located beside the tearoom, our gift shop has a number of souvenirs for you to take home.

mmarrishokk: Edinburgh Castle, 08. 01. 2016, https://znanija.com/task/16109747

Part 3: Questions 11–17

For the questions 11–17 decide if each sentence is **true** or **false** and **where** you find the information in the text. Then tick (✓) the correct box and **give the line(s) where you find the information**. You will only get a point if both parts of the answer are correct.

7 Punkte

Gentle Giants

There are many things you think of when you hear the word 'Australia': sun, surf, white sand beaches, and plenty of animals, including koalas and kangaroos. One animal that you normally don't think of is the camel. But they do exist in large herds in outback Australia. In fact, Australia's wild camel population is the biggest in the world, with about 750,000 roaming wild in the outback.

So how did they get here? Settlers introduced camels when they arrived in the 1840s. The increase in Australia's camel population developed from there. They were first used for transport over long distances in the desert.

But when technology developed and cars were invented, they weren't needed anymore. Thousands of camels were released into the wild.

Although it was a good idea to introduce camels at the time, today there are more problems than advantages. Because they're so big, they have no natural enemies. That's why the camel population increased. Camels are made for surviving in the outback, because they can eat dry and thorny plants. However, they need to drink so much water at a time, they must use the waterholes that farmers need for their animals. As water is a very rare resource in the Outback, this has become more and more of a problem in recent years.

If you travel through central Australia chances are you will see camels. They're everywhere – the biggest wild herds live in the desert regions near the borders of Western Australia, the Northern Territory and South Australia. Watch out, because they often stand on the highway and you don't want to hit one with your car!

If you won't be here for long and want to make sure you see camels, visit one of the camel farms. There are over 50 Australian camel farms, trying to attract tourists. The farms are all over the country and the camels are well kept on their farms. You can go for a ten-minute camel ride, or a three-week camel safari. You can also take a camel trip around Ayers Rock, or Uluru as the Aborigines call the mountain. You can even have a taste of camel ice-cream produced on these farms.

Caitlin Morahan: Did You Know There Are Wild Camels in Australia?, Culture Trip vom 04. 06. 2018, https://theculturetrip.com/pacific/australia/articles/did-you-know-there-are-wild-camels-in-australia/

	true	false	line(s)
0. People think about skiing when they hear the word "Australia".	☐	☑	1-2
11. There are more wild camels in Australia than everywhere else in the world.	☐	☐	______
12. Immigrants brought camels with them when they settled in Australia.	☐	☐	______
13. Later, motor vehicles replaced camels.	☐	☐	______
14. Wild animals reduce the number of camels in Australia.	☐	☐	______
15. Camels and farmers use the same water resources.	☐	☐	______
16. Camels can be a danger when you travel by car.	☐	☐	______
17. Camels are not allowed near the Aborigines' holy mountain.	☐	☐	______

Part 4: Questions 18–25

8 Punkte

Read the following article about the Fridays for Future protests. Match the first parts of the sentences (18–25) with the sentence endings (A–J).

#fridaysforfuture: Teens Changing the World

On March 15, 2019, schools worldwide were left empty as students took to the streets to protest against climate change. They wanted to get more people to talk about climate change and told their friends to spread the word on social media via #fridaysforfuture. They believe governments have not done enough to fight the Earth's warming.

These protests were among the biggest worldwide climate change actions so far. Hundreds of thousands of students protested in more than 100 countries.

The "school strikes" were organized by Greta Thunberg, a teenage activist from Sweden. She began holding protests by herself in 2018. She protested outside the Swedish government. Then more protests happened. First only a handful of cities had protests, later students in hundreds of cities joined Greta's campaign.

In Washington, D. C., speakers stood behind the sign "We don't want to die." In Berlin, Germany, as many as 20,000 protesters gathered. They marched to Chancellor Angela Merkel's office.

There were also protests in Pretoria, South Africa. More than 1 billion people live in Africa and scientists expect it to be hardest hit by warming. This is unfair because Africa is doing very little to make climate change worse. That is because there is less use of fossil fuels there than in industrialized countries. Burning these fuels creates greenhouse gases such as carbon dioxide which scientists believe to cause global warming.

Many scientists all over the world supported the protests and signed petitions backing the students. Some politicians also joined students. Denmark's Prime Minister Lars Loekke Rasmussen for example went to a protest. He tweeted that adults must listen to young people. "Especially when they're right," his tweet said.

Thunberg spoke at the protest in Stockholm on March 15th that demanded government action against climate change. She said the world faces its biggest problem ever. In the end it will be the children who will live in the world that climate change creates. She said, "Why should I be studying for a future that soon may be no more, when no one is doing anything to save that future?"

eigene Zusammenstellung nach: https://newsela.com/read/worldwide-student-climate-protest/id/50348/ (19. 03. 2019); https://www.yourweather.co.uk/news/trending/Fridays-for-the-future-uk-students-protest-for-climate-change.html (19. 03. 2019); https://fridaysforfuture.de (19. 03. 2019)

		A	that is endangered by global warming.
18	The protesters want governments	B	are one cause of global warming.
19	Teenage activist Greta Thunberg	C	agree with the students.
20	20,000 young people	D	in more than 100 countries.
21	Scientists think that greenhouse gases	E	protested in Berlin.
22	In Africa people don't use as much	F	that will have much more rain.
23	A lot of scientists and politicians	G	started the "school strike"-campaign.
24	Denmark's Prime Minister	H	fossil fuel as the rest of the world.
25	Today's children will live in a world	I	wants adults to listen to the protesters.
		J	to do more against climate change.

18.	19.	20.	21.	22.	23.	24.	25.

III. Mediating

7 Punkte

1. **Stay safe online**
Deine Schwester hat im Internet diese Verhaltenstipps gefunden. Da sie nur wenig Englisch versteht, fragt sie dich um Hilfe. Sie versteht nur die erste Regel. Erkläre ihr die Regeln 2–8 **auf Deutsch**.

8 tips to stay safe online

1. *Sei nett zu anderen Menschen, wenn du online bist.*
2. ______________________
3. ______________________
4. ______________________
5. ______________________
6. ______________________
7. ______________________
8. ______________________

2. **Gefährliches Gewässer!** 3 Punkte
Du bist mit Antonia aus Texas spazieren. Ihr seht das folgende Schild. Antonia möchte von dir wissen, was es bedeutet. Erkläre ihr das Schild **auf Englisch**.

Schild „Achtung“: © foxy cat. Shutterstock

1. ______________________________
2. ______________________________
3. ______________________________

IV. Writing: Wahlmöglichkeit 1

Part 1: AppWhats photo message – a concert

8 Punkte

You have posted this photo on AppWhats. Your friend Kevin wants to know more about the situation. Write two sentences for each part.

Cool picture, huh?

Wow, what's going on?

____

____

____

Where is it?

____

____

____

Who is with you?

____

____

How is the atmosphere? Do you like it?

____

____

____

Foto: Joel Muniz/Unsplash

Part 2: An online comment

Should students be punished for taking part in #fridaysforfuture demonstrations instead of going to school? 12 Punkte

Write
- two pros,
- two cons,
- and your opinion. (Give reasons.)

Write about **80 words**.

Words: ___________

Foto: picture alliance/dpa / Federico Gambarini

IV. Writing: Wahlmöglichkeit 2

Part 1: #fridaysforfuture workshop

8 Punkte

You want to take part in a #fridaysforfuture workshop. The organizers have sent you the following form. Fill in the form.

#fridaysforfuture workshop

First Name: ______________________

Last Name: ______________________

Date of birth: ______________________

Address with country: ______________________

____

Why do **you** want to take part in a #fridaysforfuture workshop? Give two reasons.

____

____

What do you expect from the workshop?

- ______________________
- ______________________

What does your school already do to protect the environment or what action do you plan to take at your school?

- ______________________
- ______________________

Part 2: Creative writing: A writing competition

There's a writing competition in your favourite animal magazine. They want you to write a story about this picture. 12 Punkte

Include the following aspects:
- the situation
- their relationship
- what happens next

Write about **80 words**.

Words: ____________

Kurs G

II. Reading

Part 1: Questions 1–5

5 Punkte

Read the texts below. Then read the statements (1–5).
Decide whether the statements are **true** or **false**. Then tick (✓) the correct box.

1.

To rent:
Modern flat on the
2nd floor in London SW 6

- 2 large bedrooms – not furnished – floor to ceiling windows – large open kitchen
- 2 minutes from tube station
- Shops and restaurants within walking distance
- Only £ 850 a month!
- Viewing anytime that suits you

Phone 020 933 9458

2.

We buy your phone!

Got a new smartphone? Great!

Why not sell your old one?
We buy all brands and models.

BEST PRICES PAID!

For more information visit our webpage:
www.webuyyourphone.com

3.

4.

Teen Writing Club

For kids in grades 6–10

September 18th – December 18th (no class Nov 6th)

Tuesdays 4 pm – 5 pm

Do you like to write and want to share your stories, poems or thoughts?

We meet every Tuesday this fall at the Spencer Library. Let's write some great texts.

For more information email to *inspiration@spencer-library.com*

Spencer Library, 244 East Street, New York

	true	false
1. The people from *webuyyourphone.com* are interested in new phones.	☐	☐
2. The two-bedroom flat is only two minutes from shops and restaurants.	☐	☐
3. The Rhema Theatre Company puts a show together in less than a week.	☐	☐
4. The teen writing club takes place every Tuesday during the summer.	☐	☐
5. Young writers can't write poems at the library on the 6th November.	☐	☐

Part 2: Questions 6–10

Edinburgh Castle

Read these short texts about Edinburgh Castle and decide which headline (A–G) fits each text (6–10) best.
Write the correct letters behind the numbers.

5 Punkte

A	A lot to see
B	Used by the army
C	Home to royalty
D	Ancient traditions live on
E	Treat yourself
F	A national symbol
G	Get a tattoo

6. ☐ Edinburgh Castle, which is high above the city on Castle Rock, was once the home of the kings and queens of Scotland. The 700-year-old Crown of Scotland can still be seen there. James I, who later became King of England, was born there in 1566.
7. ☐ Many battles with the English took place at the castle. It was attacked many times over the centuries but was never destroyed. That is why many Scots see it as a symbol of their own survival.
8. ☐ Visitors to the Castle will see a military guard at the gate, because the castle is still the headquarters of the Scottish part of the army. Every August the famous *Military Tattoo* takes place here. This is a great three-week festival of bagpipe[1] and band music.
9. ☐ In Edinburgh Castle you can see exhibitions of Scottish history and a collection of armour and weapons. There are lots of interesting things to see inside and outside the castle. The hilltop position also offers the best view of the city of Edinburgh.
10. ☐ The traditional afternoon teas can be a highlight of your visit to the castle. Enjoy sandwiches, scones, home-baked cake and tea. Our gift shop next to the tea room has a number of souvenirs for you to take home.

1 bagpipes = Dudelsack

mmarrishokk: Edinburgh Castle, 08. 01. 2016, https://znanija.com/task/16109747

Part 3: Questions 11–17

7 Punkte

For the questions 11–17 decide if each sentence is **true** or **false** and **where** you find the information in the text. Then tick (✓) the correct box and **give the line(s) where you find the information**. You will only get a point if both parts of the answer are correct.

Gentle Giants

There are many things you think of when you hear the word 'Australia': sun, surf, white sand beaches, and plenty of animals, including koalas and kangaroos. One animal that you normally don't think of is the camel. But they do exist in large herds in outback Australia. In fact, Australia's wild camel population is the biggest in the world, with about 750,000 roaming wild in the outback.

So how did they get here? Settlers took camels with them on their journey to Australia in the 1840s. They were first used to transport goods over long distances in the desert.

After cars were invented, they weren't needed anymore. Thousands of camels were set free into the wild.

Although it was a good idea to introduce camels at the time, today there are more problems than advantages. Because they're so big, they have no natural enemies. That's why there are so many camels now. Camels are made for living in the outback, because they can eat dry and thorny plants. However, they need to drink so much water at a time, they must use the waterholes that farmers need for their animals. Today this is a problem because there is not enough water in the outback.

If you travel through central Australia, you will probably see camels. They're everywhere – the biggest wild herds live in the desert regions near the borders of Western Australia, the Northern Territory and South Australia. Watch out, because they often stand on the highway and you don't want to hit one with your car!

If you want to make sure you see camels, visit one of the camel farms. There are over 50 Australian camel farms all over the country where all the camels are well kept. To do something special you can go for a ten-minute camel ride, or a three-week camel safari. You can also take a camel trip around Ayers Rock, or Uluru as the Aborigines call the mountain. You can even have a taste of camel ice-cream produced on these farms.

Caitlin Morahan: Did You Know There Are Wild Camels in Australia?, Culture Trip vom 04. 06. 2018, https://theculturetrip.com/pacific/australia/articles/did-you-know-there-are-wild-camels-in-australia/

Foto: © Standards Australia/CC BY 3.0 AU

	true	false	line(s)
0. People think about skiing when they hear the word "Australia".	☐	☑	1-2
11. There are more wild camels in Australia than everywhere else in the world.	☐	☐	______
12. Settlers brought camels with them when they came to Australia.	☐	☐	______
13. Later, motor vehicles replaced camels.	☐	☐	______
14. Wild animals reduce the number of camels in Australia.	☐	☐	______
15. Camels and farmers use the same waterholes.	☐	☐	______
16. Camels can be a danger when you travel by car.	☐	☐	______
17. Camels are not allowed near the Aborigines' holy mountain.	☐	☐	______

Part 4: Questions 18–25

Read the following article about the Fridays for Future protests. Match the first parts of the sentences (18–25) with the sentence endings (A–J).

8 Punkte

#fridaysforfuture: Teens Changing the World

On March 15, 2019, schools worldwide were left empty as students protested against climate change. They wanted more people to talk about climate change and told their friends to write about it on social media. They think governments have not done enough to fight the Earth's warming.

These protests have been some of the biggest worldwide climate change actions so far. Hundreds of thousands of students protested in more than 100 countries.

The "school strikes" were organized by Greta Thunberg, a teenage activist from Sweden. She began to protest in 2018 outside the Swedish government. Then more protests happened. First only a handful of cities had protests, later students in hundreds of cities joined Greta's campaign.

In Washington, D.C., speakers stood behind the sign "We don't want to die." In Berlin, Germany, as many as 20,000 protesters marched to Chancellor Angela Merkel's office.

There were also protests in Pretoria, South Africa. More than 1 billion people live in Africa and scientists expect that Africans will have the biggest problems with global warming. This is unfair because Africa is doing very little to make climate change worse. That is because Africa uses less fossil fuels than industrialized countries. Burning these fuels creates greenhouse gases such as carbon dioxide. Many scientists say these gases can cause global warming. That is why they supported the protests and signed petitions.

Some politicians also joined students. Denmark's Prime Minister Lars Loekke Rasmussen for example went to a protest. He tweeted that adults must listen to young people. "Especially when they're right," his tweet said.

Thunberg spoke at the protest in Stockholm on March 15th that asked governments for action against climate change. She said the world faces its biggest problem ever. In the end it will be the children who will live in the world that climate change creates. She said, "Why should I be studying for a future that soon may be no more, when no one is doing anything to save that future?"

eigene Zusammenstellung nach: https://newsela.com/read/worldwide-student-climate-protest/id/50348/ (19.03.2019); https://www.yourweather.co.uk/news/trending/Fridays-for-the-future-uk-students-protest-for-climate-change.html (19.03.2019); https://fridaysforfuture.de (19.03.2019)

		A	that will have much more rain.
18	The protesters want governments	B	fossil fuel as the rest of the world.
19	Teenage activist Greta Thunberg	C	are one cause of global warming
20	20,000 young people	D	that is in danger because of global warming.
21	Scientists think that greenhouse gases	E	wants adults to listen to the protesters.
22	In Africa people don't use as much	F	started the "school strike"-campaign.
23	A lot of scientists and politicians	G	to do more against climate change.
24	Denmark's Prime Minister	H	agree with the students.
25	Today's children will live in a world	I	protested in Berlin.

18.	19.	20.	21.	22.	23.	24.	25.

III. Mediating

1. **Stay safe online** 7 Punkte

Deine Schwester hat im Internet diese Verhaltenstipps gefunden. Da sie nur wenig Englisch versteht, fragt sie dich um Hilfe. Sie versteht nur die erste Regel. Erkläre ihr die Regeln 1–7 **auf Deutsch**.

7 tips to stay safe online

1. ______________________________
2. ______________________________
3. ______________________________
4. ______________________________
5. ______________________________
6. ______________________________
7. ______________________________

3 Punkte

2. **Gefährliches Gewässer!**
Du bist mit Antonia aus Texas an einem See spazieren. Ihr seht das folgende Schild. Antonia möchte von dir wissen, was es bedeutet. Erkläre ihr das Schild **auf Englisch**.

Schild „Achtung“: © foxy cat. Shutterstock

1. ______________________________
2. ______________________________
3. ______________________________

IV. Writing: Set 1

Part 1: AppWhats photo message – a concert

8 Punkte

You have posted this photo on AppWhats. Your friend Kevin wants to know more about the situation. Write two sentences for each part.

Cool picture, huh?

Wow, what's going on?

___

Where is it?

___

Who is with you?

___

How is the atmosphere? Do you like it?

___

Foto: Joel Muniz/Unsplash

Part 2: An online comment

12 Punkte Should students be punished for taking part in #fridaysforfuture demonstrations instead of going to school?

Write
- two pros,
- two cons,
- and your opinion. (Give reasons.)

Write about **60 words**.

Words: ___________

Foto: picture alliance/dpa / Federico Gambarini

IV. Writing: Set II

Part 1: #fridaysforfuture workshop

You want to take part in a #fridaysforfuture workshop. The organizers have sent you the following form. Fill in the form.

8 Punkte

#fridaysforfuture workshop

First Name: ______________________

Family Name: ______________________

Date of birth: ______________________

Address with country: ______________________

____

Why do **you** want to take part in a #fridaysforfuture workshop? Give two reasons.

____

____

What are **you** doing in your everyday life to save our planet?

- ______________________
- ______________________

What does your school do to protect the environment or what could your school do?

- ______________________
- ______________________

Part 2: Creative writing: A writing competition

12 Punkte

There's a writing competition in your favourite animal magazine. They want you to write a story about this picture.

Include the following aspects:

- the situation
- their relationship
- what happens next

Write about **60 words**.

____

Words: __________

Hauptschulabschlussprüfung Niedersachsen
Englisch 2021

Kurse E und G

I. Listening

Part 1: Questions 1–7

Worksheet
7 Punkte

You will hear seven short conversations.
You will hear each conversation twice.
For each question there are three pictures and a short recording.
Choose the correct picture and put a tick (✓) in the box below it.

Example:

0. Which tickets do they buy?

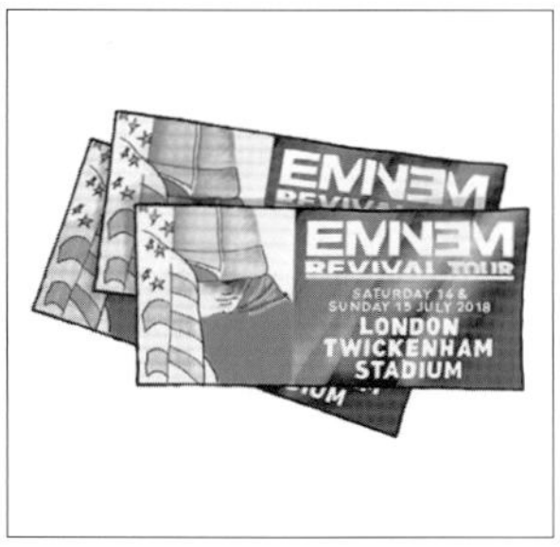

A ☐

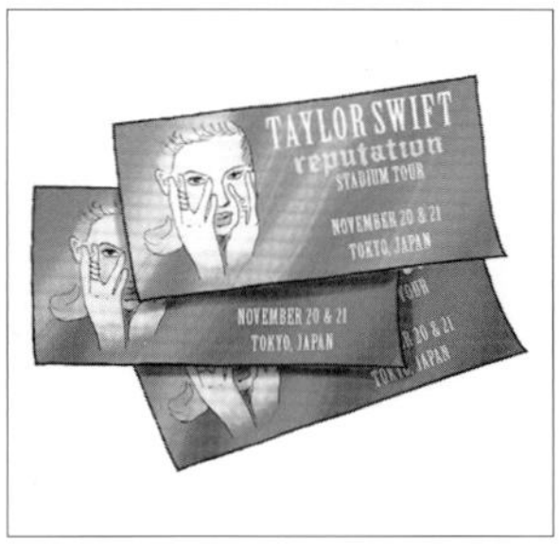

B ☐

C ☑

1. When does the training take place?

A ☐

B ☐

C ☐

2. Which film do they want to watch?

A ☐

B ☐

C ☐

3. Which main course do they order?

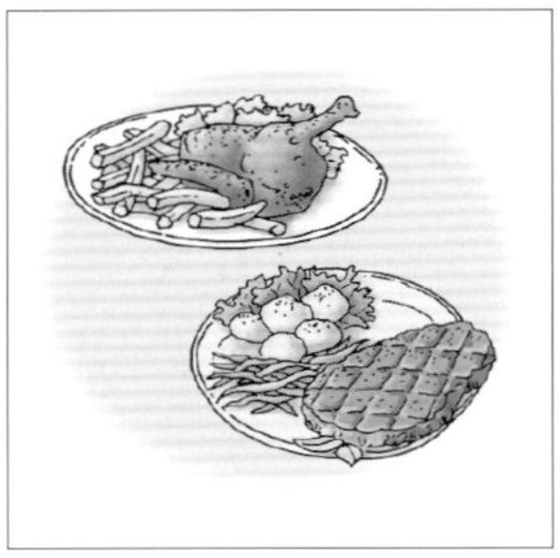

A ☐ B ☐ C ☐

4. What problem does the man have?

A ☐ B ☐ C ☐

5. Which road should you take into London?

A ☐ B ☐ C ☐

6. At what time do the women meet?

A ☐ B ☐ C ☐

7. What kind of music will they have at their graduation party?

A ☐

B ☐

C ☐

Kurs E

Part 2: Questions 8–13

After the school lockdown

6 Punkte

Listen to the following conversation between Grace, a 15-year-old high school student from Bristol, and her grandmother. Grace is talking about her experiences with distance learning during the COVID-19 school lockdown.
For questions 8–13 tick (✓) the correct box A, B or C.
The first question is an example.

Example:

0. Grace talks to …
   - A Mrs. Tomlinson. ☐
   - B her grandmother. ☑
   - C her sister Emma. ☐

8. For Grace the worst thing during the school lockdown was …
   - A wearing a mask. ☐
   - B not going to school. ☐
   - C not seeing her friends. ☐

9. After returning to school …
   - A they have to wear face masks. ☐
   - B not a lot has changed. ☐
   - C the students do a lot of group work. ☐

10. During the lockdown, Grace …
   - A spent less time on the computer than before. ☐
   - B was sometimes happy to turn off the screen. ☐
   - C became a screen addict. ☐

11. Grace preferred …
   - A filling out worksheets as usual. ☐
   - B getting work back and correcting the mistakes. ☐
   - C working at her own speed. ☐

12. Grace really enjoyed …
   - A the virtual forest walk with her biology teacher. ☐
   - B taking pictures of plants and insects. ☐
   - C talking to a nature guide about plants and insects. ☐

13. Emma freaked out because she ...
A got her mobile phone earlier than Grace. ☐
B deleted her work one day. ☐
C had to do online work. ☐

Kurs G

Part 2: Questions 8–13

After the school lockdown

6 Punkte

Listen to the following conversation between Grace, a 15-year-old high school student from Bristol, and her grandmother. Grace is talking about her experiences with distance learning during the COVID-19 school lockdown.
For questions 8–13 tick (✓) the correct box A, B or C.
The first question is an example.

Example:

0. Grace talks to ...
A Mrs. Tomlinson. ☐
B her grandmother. ☑
C her sister Emma. ☐

8. During the school lockdown Grace hated ...
A wearing a mask. ☐
B not going to school. ☐
C not seeing her friends. ☐

9. After going back to school ...
A they have to wear face masks. ☐
B nothing has changed. ☐
C the students do a lot of group work. ☐

10. During the lock-down, Grace ...
A spent less time on the computer than before. ☐
B was sometimes happy to turn off the screen. ☐
C became a screen addict[1]. ☐

11. Grace preferred ...
A filling out worksheets as usual. ☐
B correcting the mistakes in her work. ☐
C working at her own speed. ☐

12. Grace really enjoyed ...
A the virtual walk through the forest. ☐
B taking pictures for a biology project. ☐
C talking to a nature guide. ☐

13. Emma freaked out because ...
A she got her mobile phone earlier than Grace. ☐
B she deleted her work one day. ☐
C she had to do online work. ☐

1 screen addict – jemand, der süchtig nach Computern/Handys ist

Kurs E

Part 3: Questions 14–21

Mushroom coconut noodles

Listen to this cooking podcast. Ella is going to describe how she prepares mushroom coconut noodles. For questions 14–21, fill in the gaps to complete the notes. The first question is an example.

8 Punkte

0	This podcast is an episode of	*Ella cooks easy food.*
14	First you slice	______ mushrooms
15	Mushrooms will be soft after	______
16	To make it yummy add	______ and
17		______
18	For sweetness, add	______
19	Ella thinks the dish is the perfect	______
20	Another vegetable Ella suggests is	______
21	Preparation time	______

Kurs G

Part 3: Questions 14–21

Mushroom coconut noodles

Listen to this cooking podcast. Ella is going to describe how she prepares mushroom coconut noodles. For questions 14–21, fill in the gaps to complete the notes. The first question is an example.

8 Punkte

0	This podcast is an episode of	*Ella cooks easy food.*
14	First you slice a pack of	______
15	You fry the mushrooms with some oil,	______ and ______
16	To make it yummy add half a can of	______
17	and two teaspoons of	______
18	For sweetness, add a little bit of	______
19	To spice it up add a tiny bit of	______

20	When it's ready, mix the sauce with	____________________
21	Preparation time	____________________

Kurs E

Part 4: Questions 22–27

Why Germany is a great place to live

6 Punkte

You will hear a radio interview with Noah Clarkson, an American teenager who has just returned from a year in Germany as an exchange student.
For questions 22–27 decide whether each sentence is true or false.
Put a tick (✓) in the correct box 'true' or 'false'.
The first question is an example.

		true	false
0.	Emily Sanders spent a year in Germany.	☐	☑
22.	Noah's great-grandfather moved from America to Germany.	☐	☐
23.	Noah says that there is good public transportation in the US.	☐	☐
24.	Traveling on a bus in Germany is a practical way to get around.	☐	☐
25.	Noah traveled to other cities in Europe.	☐	☐
26.	In Germany people prefer traditional food to international food.	☐	☐
27.	Noah is going to Germany this summer.	☐	☐

Kurs G

Part 4: Questions 22–27

Why Germany is a great place to live

6 Punkte

You will hear a radio interview with Noah Clarkson, an American teenager who has just returned from a year in Germany as an exchange student.
For questions 22–27 decide whether each sentence is true or false.
Put a tick (✓) in the correct box 'true' or 'false'.
The first question is an example.

		true	false
0.	Emily Sanders spent a year in Germany.	☐	☑
22.	Noah's great grandfather still lives in Germany.	☐	☐
23.	Noah says that public transportation in the US is very good.	☐	☐
24.	Using a bus in Germany is a quick and easy way to get around.	☐	☐
25.	Noah went to other cities in Europe.	☐	☐
26.	Traditional food is more popular in Germany than international food.	☐	☐
27.	Noah is going to visit his German friends this summer.	☐	☐

Kurs E

II. Reading

Part 1: Questions 1–7

Read the texts below. Then read the statements (1–7).
Decide whether the statements are **true** or **false**. Then tick (✓) the correct box.

7 Punkte

1.

Lost – Help me find my blue Fiat Panda 1.2

I ran out of petrol and parked it on the side of the road. Stupidly I did not make a note of the road name.

If anyone spots a blue **FIAT PANDA**, **Registration KS63 VFW**, I would be very grateful for a hint.
A taxi picked me up at the bottom of the road and it was about a 30-minute drive back to Kingston where I live.

Contact JOHN 079417598348

2.

Cooking Class
Sign up for this free cooking class. You will learn how to prepare healthy meals.

Cooking classes offer:
- Delicious recipes
- Cooking supplies
- Shopping tips

Sign up information:
Dates: Wednesday, Jan. 15, Feb. 19, Mar. 18,
Time: 5 - 6:30 pm

Location: Family Health Center
Classes taught in English and Spanish

3.

LITERATURE FOR YOUNG ADULTS

MONDAYS & WEDNESDAYS

3-4:20PM

PROF. EMERY PETCHAUER

In this reading course students will read young adult literature. We will read several books. Hip-hop, time-travel, zombies and magical creatures will be in the mix as well as films and TV series about strong young characters.

SPRING 2021 Reading load: about 1 book/week

4.

SHOP SAFELY
AT YOUR FARMERS MARKET!

Help us practice safe and healthy shopping for all during the COVID-19 Pandemic.

NO CONTACT

- pay by card or use exact change if possible
- put your shopping into shopping bags yourself

HANDWASHING

- use hand washing stations before entering the market
- wash your hands regularly while shopping

THANK YOU FOR YOUR HELP!

		true	false
1.	You must speak Spanish to join the cooking class.	☐	☐
2.	At the Farmers Market they will put your shopping into bags for you.	☐	☐
3.	John can't remember where he parked his car.	☐	☐
4.	In the literature class for young adults they will also show films.	☐	☐
5.	You can wash your hands before you enter the Farmers Market.	☐	☐
6.	John's car is parked about 30 minutes away from where he lives.	☐	☐
7.	You must bring your own cooking supplies.	☐	☐

Part 2: Questions 8–14

7 ways to minimize your carbon footprint

7 Punkte

Seven young people are speaking about ways they found to minimize their carbon footprint. For speakers 8–14 choose the correct statement A–I.
Write the correct letter (A–I) in the box next to the number. There are more statements than speakers. Each letter can only be used once.

A	**Find "greener" ways to get around.**
B	**Take your own bag with you when shopping.**
C	**Change the way you consume.**
D	**Consume less meat.**
E	**Plant more trees.**
F	**Say no to plastic water bottles.**
G	**Travel wisely – fly less.**
H	**Unplug any electronics you're not using.**
I	**Reduce water use.**

8. ☐  **Rita:** My Mum used to bring back loads of plastic bags whenever she went shopping. A few months ago, we decided to take our own shopping basket or bag with us when we go to the shops. The few times we forgot that and had to use a plastic bag, we at least made sure we reused it several times before we used it as a bin liner.

9. ☐  **Ben:** I have gone vegan. Did you know that it takes over 5 000 gallons of water to produce a single pound of beef? And that cows and sheep produce a lot of methane gas, which has a massive impact on global warming? I mean, not eating any meat was difficult but there are so many nice alternatives. You could start with a single vegan day, maybe a "Meatless Monday".

10. ☐  **Annie:** Whenever possible, unplug your electronic devices – TVs, computers or mobile phones because even when they're switched off, or all charged up, they're consuming energy. And since electricity production accounts for over 37 % of carbon dioxide emissions in the United States, unplugging is the way to go.

11. ☐  **Joan:** You hear it all the time "Plastic is bad!". Loads of the stuff ends up in landfills or even in the ocean where animals are badly affected by it. There are ways to use less plastic – I invested in a reusable water bottle and always carry it with

me. There are many other things that are made from plastic and can easily be replaced by more sustainable alternatives.

12. ☐ 

Harry: I just got my driver's licence. But I am still not taking the car to go to school. Taking the bus or cycling is fine for me. I try not to use the car so much because how you get from A to B has a significant environmental impact. Walking, biking or taking public transport are all better than driving your car.

13. ☐ 

Bob: Buy fewer things and consume less. Recycle wherever possible, or reuse things. If you buy, buy high-quality things and make them last. You don't always need the latest mobile, try to use yours as long as possible or sell it on. It's important to save resources this way to reduce the impact on your carbon footprint.

14. ☐ 

Sandra: Don't let your water consumption run out of control! You can save up to 60 liters of water every week by turning off your tap while you brush your teeth. Every minute you spend in a shower uses up to 17 liters of water. Also, washing a full machine of clothes uses less water and energy than two half loads.

Part 3: Questions 15–21

For questions 15–21 tick (✓) the correct box **true** or **false** and **give the line(s) where you find the information**. You will only get a point if both parts of the answer are correct.

7 Punkte

Fake News

When you are online, you often see unwanted pictures, articles, links and videos trying to tell you their story. Often these stories are not true even though they sound and look like they could be. They have been specifically written to catch your interest and make you click on a story or an ad on another website. And sometimes those stories even tell lies to upset people for political reasons. This kind of news stories circulates quickly, and the result is fake news. Read these experts' tips to know when news is fake news and don't get fooled!

First of all, check the source: Look at the website where you found the story. Does it look real? Is the text well-written? Fake news websites often use web addresses (URL) that sound like real newspapers, but don't have many real stories about other topics.

Second, you should watch out for fake photos. Many fake news stories use photoshopped images. Sometimes, if you look closely at an image, you can see that it has been changed. So be careful and check the pictures.

Check if the story you are reading is on other news sites, too. If you find it on a number of other sites, then it probably isn't fake. Also find out about the website's sources. Serious news organizations check their sources before they publish a story.

Obviously, there are other signs for fake news. There are many techniques that fake news uses. For example, using ALL CAPS (and lots of ads that pop up when you click on a link). Also, think about how the story makes you feel. If the news story makes you angry, it's probably designed to do so.

If you know these things about online news, and use them in your everyday life, then you have control over what to read, what to believe and most importantly what to share. If you find a news story that you know is fake: don't share it!

How to spot fake news, https://learnenglish.britishcouncil.org/skills/reading/intermediate-b1/how-to-spot-fake-news

		true	false	line(s)
0.	This article is about fake news.	☑	☐	1
15.	Fake news looks like real news.	☐	☐	______
16.	Fake news is designed to get your attention.	☐	☐	______
17.	It's important to find out where the story comes from.	☐	☐	______
18.	Fake news websites always use original photos.	☐	☐	______
19.	You can find the same fake news on many different news sites.	☐	☐	______
20.	Some stories want to make you angry.	☐	☐	______
21.	You shouldn't send fake news to other people.	☐	☐	______

Part 4: Questions 22–28

7 Punkte

Read the following article about the history of fish and chips. Match the first parts of the sentences (22–28) with the sentence endings (A–I). There are more sentence endings than you need.

The story of fish and chips

Long before the Big Mac was invented, Britain had its own national form of fast food.

"When I was a young man, it was great to have fish and chips once or twice a week," remembers 82-year-old Arthur Mowbrey. "Sixty years ago, you'd get a full-size portion of cod and chips for only a few pennies. It was cheap, and good. Every town in Britain had its fish'n'chip shops."

For a hundred years, they were the classic popular take-aways, British style. You could eat fish and chips in the street on your way home from work, or during the lunchbreak. Wrapped in newspaper, it would keep warm. Fresh sea fish could easily be bought in many British towns because they are near a port. Cheaper than meat, sea fish became a popular source of protein.

Things have changed. "Today young people prefer hamburgers or other take-away," says Lizzie, a teenager. "Fish'n'chips is a bit old-fashioned. But there are still cheap chip shops around. We sometimes have it at home, and we go and get it from the chip shop. It saves cooking!"

Thousands of chip shops have closed in the last twenty-five years. Some shops have survived in seaside towns, where the fish is really fresh. Traditionally, people visit them and eat there. Fish'n'chips wrapped in newspaper is already just a memory of the past. British and European hygiene rules no longer allow food to be wrapped in old papers, so today's carry-out chip shops use new paper or plastic boxes.

Fish and chips will survive as a specialty. Comfortable, more expensive fish restaurants with tables and chairs have existed for a long time. In the years to come, they may be the only type of fish'n'chip restaurant around.

No more fish'n'chips?, https://linguapress.com/intermediate/fish-chips.htm

		A	you don't have to cook.
22.	Many years ago, fish and chips	B	had fish and chips every week.
23.	When he was a young man, Arthur Mowbrey	C	eat fish and chips in restaurants where they can sit down.
24.	Fish and chips	D	were wrapped in a newspaper.
25.	Sea fish, a popular source of protein,	E	you can buy really fresh fish.
26.	In towns on the coast	F	invented the Big Mac.
27.	If you buy take-away fish and chips	G	keep you warm.
28.	In the future people will	H	is a typical British fast food.
		I	used to cost less than meat.

22.	23.	24.	25.	26.	27.	28.

III. Writing: Set I

Part 1: AppWhats photo message: Summer holidays in Australia

10 Punkte

You are on holiday in Australia and send this picture to your friend Marc. He wants to know more about your holiday.

Great picture, huh?
Greetings from Australia!
Having a great time here!
See you soon!

Marc: Thank you! Are you there on holiday? Who is with you?

You: ______________________________

Marc: How was your flight?

You: ______________________________

Marc: What cool animals have you seen so far?

You: ______________________________

Marc: What places have you been to? What else do you want to see?

You: ______________________________

Marc: Have you planned any cool activities?

You: ______________________________

Marc: And where are you staying?

You: ______________________________

Marc: When will you be back? Can we meet up? I would love to see more pictures!

You: ______________________________

Bild: © twobluedogs. 123rf.com

Part 2: Write a comment: Voluntary work

Helping at an animal shelter, working for the fire brigade or supporting a social or ecological project at school – spend your free time working for a good cause! Become a volunteer!

15 Punkte

Can you imagine spending your free time with voluntary work?

Give
- two pros,
- two cons,
- and your opinion. (Give reasons.)

Write about **80 words**.

Words: ____________

III. Writing: Set II

Part 1: Questionnaire: Smartphones in school

10 Punkte

You are spending a year abroad in London. Your school wants to allow students to use their smartphones in school. Help them to organise it by filling in the questionnaire.

Smartphones in school

How could you use your smartphone as an additional tool in class?
Give two examples.

- ____________________
- ____________________

Would you like to use your phone during breaks? Give two reasons.

☐ Yes ☐ No

- ____________________
- ____________________

Name two disadvantages of using your phone in school and explain them.

- ____________________
- ____________________

Should there be a mobile free zone in school? Say where and why or why not.

____

____

Give two rules for using the smartphone in school safely.

- ____________________
- ____________________

Part 2: Creative writing: The cave

15 Punkte

I was standing in front of the cave's entrance. Around the cave there were several different signs warning people to keep out. I wondered what could be in there. I had a torch, so …

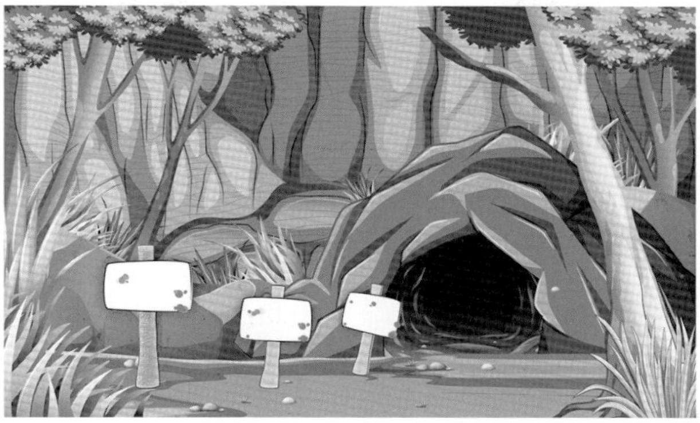

adapted: © BlueRingMedia/Shutterstock

Complete the story.

Include the following aspects:

- what the signs said
- what was in the cave
- what happened next

Write about **80 words**.

Words: ____________

Kurs G

II. Reading

Part 1: Questions 1–7

7 Punkte

Read the texts below. Then read the statements (1–7).
Decide whether the statements are **true** or **false**. Then tick (✓) the correct box.

1.

Lost – Help me find my blue Fiat Panda 1.2

I have lost my Blue Fiat Panda. I parked it on the side of a road and don't remember the road name. It is parked about a 30-minute drive away from my home in Kingston.

If you see a blue **FIAT PANDA**, **Registration KS63 VFW**, please call me.

Contact JOHN 079417598348

2.

Cooking Class
Sign up for this free cooking class. You will learn how to prepare healthy meals.

Cooking classes offer:
- Delicious recipes
- Cooking supplies
- Shopping tips

Sign up information:
Dates: Wednesday, Jan. 15, Feb. 19, Mar. 18,
Time: 5 - 6:30 pm
Location: Family Health Center
Classes taught in English and Spanish
Interested?
Call 847-666-2425

3.

LITERATURE FOR YOUNG ADULTS

MONDAYS & WEDNESDAYS

3-4:20PM

PROF. EMERY PETCHAUER

SPRING 2021

In this reading course students will read young adult literature. We will read several books. Topics will include Hip-hop, time-travel, zombies and magical creatures. We will also watch films and TV series about strong young characters.

Reading load: about 1 book/week

4.

SHOP SAFELY
AT YOUR FARMERS MARKET!
Help us practice safe and healthy shopping for all during the COVID-19 Pandemic.

NO CONTACT
- pay by card or use exact change if possible
- put your shopping into shopping bags yourself

HANDWASHING
- use hand washing stations before entering the market
- wash your hands regularly while shopping

THANK YOU FOR YOUR HELP!

		true	false
1.	You must speak Spanish to join the cooking class.	☐	☐
2.	At the Farmers Market they will put your shopping into bags for you.	☐	☐
3.	John can't remember where he parked his car.	☐	☐
4.	In the literature class for young adults they will also show films.	☐	☐
5.	You can wash your hands before you enter the Farmers Market.	☐	☐
6.	John's car is parked about 30 minutes away from where he lives.	☐	☐
7.	You must bring your own cooking supplies.	☐	☐

Part 2: Questions 8–14

7 ways to minimize your carbon footprint

Seven young people are speaking about ways they found to minimize their carbon footprint. For speakers 8–14 choose the correct statement (A–H). Write the correct letter (A–H) in the box next to the number. There is one more statement than speakers. Each letter can only be used once.

7 Punkte

A	**Find "greener" ways to get around.**
B	**Take your own bag with you when shopping.**
C	**Change the way you consume.**
D	**Eat less meat.**
E	**Say no to plastic water bottles.**
F	**Travel wisely – fly less.**
G	**Unplug any electronics you're not using.**
H	**Use less water.**

8. ☐ 

Rita: My Mum always brought home lots of plastic bags from the shops. A few months ago, we decided to take our own bags with us when we go to the shops. If we have to use plastic bags, we make sure we reuse them as often as possible before throwing them out.

9. ☐ 

Ben: I have gone vegan. Did you know that it takes over 5 000 gallons of water to produce a single pound of beef? I mean, not eating any meat was difficult at first but now I hardly miss it. There are so many nice alternatives. Just try it! If you want, you can start with a single vegan day.

10. ☐ 

Annie: Whenever possible, unplug your electronic devices – TVs, computers or mobile phones. Even when they're switched off, or all charged up, they're consuming energy. Over 37 % of carbon dioxide emissions in the United States are the result of electricity production.

11. ☐ 

Joan: You hear it all the time "Plastic is bad!". Loads of the stuff ends up in the ocean where animals are badly affected by it. There are ways to use less plastic – I bought a reusable water bottle and always carry it with me. There are many other things that are made from plastic and can easily be replaced.

12. ☐  **Harry:** I just got my driver's licence. But I am still not taking the car to go to school. Taking the bus or cycling is fine for me. I try not to use the car so much because how you get from A to B has a big impact on the environment. Walking, biking or taking public transport are all better than driving your car.

13. ☐  **Bob:** Buy fewer things and consume less. Recycle wherever possible or reuse things. Buy high-quality things and make them last. Try to use your mobile as long as possible or sell it on. This way you help to reduce the impact on your carbon footprint. For example, when I don't like my clothes anymore, I try to sell them or give them away to charity.

14. ☐  **Sandra:** Don't waste water! You can save up to 60 liters of water every week by turning off your tap while you brush your teeth. Every minute you spend in a shower uses up to 17 liters of water. Also, washing a full machine of clothes uses less water and energy than two half loads.

Part 3: Questions 15–21

7 Punkte

For questions 15–21 tick (✓) the correct box **true** or **false** and **give the line(s) where you find the information**. You will only get a point if both parts of the answer are correct.

Fake News

When you are online, you often see unwanted pictures, articles, links and videos trying to tell you their story. Often these stories are not true but they sound and look like they could be. They have been written to catch your interest and make you click on a story or an ad on another website. And sometimes those stories even tell lies. This kind of news stories goes around quickly, and the result is fake news. Read these experts' tips to know when news is fake news and don't get fooled!

First of all, check the source: Look at the website where you found the story. Does it look real? Is the text well-written? Fake news websites often use addresses that look like real newspapers, but don't have many real stories about other topics.

Second, you should watch out for fake photos. Many fake news stories use photoshopped images. Sometimes, if you just look closely at an image, you can see if it has been changed.

Check if the story you are reading is on other news sites, too. If you find the same story on a number of different sites, then it probably isn't fake. Also, find out about the website's sources. Serious news organizations check their sources before they publish a story.

Obviously, there are other signs for fake news. There are many techniques that fake news uses. For example, using ALL CAPS – writing everything in capital letters. Also, think about how the story makes you feel. If the news story makes you angry, it's probably been written to do so.

If you know these things about online news, then you have control over what to read, what to believe and what to share. If you find a news story that you know is fake: don't share it!

How to spot fake news, https://learnenglish.britishcouncil.org/skills/reading/intermediate-b1/how-to-spot-fake-news

	true	false	line(s)
0. This article is about fake news.	☑	☐	1
15. Fake news looks like real news.	☐	☐	______
16. Experts can show you how to spot fake news.	☐	☐	______
17. It is important to find out where the story comes from.	☐	☐	______
18. Fake news websites always use original photos.	☐	☐	______
19. You can find the same fake news on many different news sites.	☐	☐	______
20. Some stories want to make you angry.	☐	☐	______
21. You shouldn't send fake news to other people.	☐	☐	______

Part 4: Questions 22–28

7 Punkte

Read the following article about the history of fish and chips. Match the first parts of the sentences (22–28) with the sentence endings (A–H). There is one more sentence ending than you need.

The story of fish and chips

Long before the Big Mac was invented, Britain had its own national form of fast food.

"When I was a young man, it was great to have fish and chips once or twice a week," remembers 82-year-old Arthur Mowbrey. "Sixty years ago, you'd get a full-size portion of fish and chips for only a few pennies. It was cheap, and good. Every town in Britain had its fish'n'chip shops."

For a hundred years, they were the classic popular take-aways, British style. You could eat fish and chips in the street on your way home from work, or during the lunchbreak. Wrapped in newspaper, it would keep warm. You could buy fresh sea fish in many British towns because they are near a port. Cheaper than meat, sea fish became very popular.

Things have changed. "Today young people prefer hamburgers or other take-away," says Lizzie, a teenager. "Fish'n'chips is a bit old-fashioned. But there are still cheap chip shops around. We sometimes have it at home, and we go and get it from the chip shop. It saves cooking!"

Thousands of chip shops have closed in the last twenty-five years. Some shops have survived in seaside towns, where the fish is really fresh. Traditionally, people visit them and eat there. Fish'n'chips wrapped in newspaper is just a memory of the past. Hygiene rules no longer allow this. Today take-away chip shops use new paper or plastic boxes.

Fish and chips will survive as a specialty. Comfortable, more expensive fish restaurants with tables and chairs have existed for a long time. In the years to come, they may be the only type of fish'n'chip restaurant around.

No more fish'n'chips?, https://linguapress.com/intermediate/fish-chips.htm

		A	had fish and chips every week.
22	Many years ago, fish and chips	B	eat fish and chips in restaurants where they can sit down.
23	When he was a young man, Arthur Mowbrey	C	invented the Big Mac.
24	Fish and chips	D	you can buy really fresh fish.
25	Sea fish	E	were wrapped in a newspaper.
26	In towns on the coast	F	you don't have to cook.
27	If you buy take-away fish and chips	G	is a typical British fast food.
28	In the future people will	H	used to cost less than meat.

22.	23.	24.	25.	26.	27.	28.

III. Writing: Set I

Part 1: AppWhats photo message: Summer holidays in Australia

10 Punkte

You are on holiday in Australia and send this picture to your friend Marc. He wants to know more about your holiday.

Great picture, huh?
Greetings from Australia!
Having a great time here!
See you soon!

Marc: Thank you! Are you there on holiday? Who is with you?

You: ______________________________

____

Marc: How was your flight?

You: ______________________________

____

Marc: What cool animals have you seen so far?

You: ______________________________

____

Marc: What places have you been to? What else do you want to see?

You: ______________________________

____

Marc: Have you planned any cool activities?

You: ______________________________

____

Marc: And where are you staying?

You: ______________________________

____

Marc: When will you be back? Can we meet up? I would love to see more pictures!

You: ______________________________

____

Part 2: Write a comment: Voluntary work

15 Punkte

Helping at an animal shelter, working for the fire brigade or supporting a social or ecological project at school – spend your free time working for a good cause! Become a volunteer!

Can you imagine spending your free time with voluntary work?

Give
- arguments for and against voluntary work
- your opinion. (Give reasons.)

Write about **60 words**.

Words: ___________

III. Writing: Set II

Part 1: Questionnaire: Smartphones in school

You are spending a year abroad in London. Your school wants to allow students to use their smartphones in school. Help them to organise it by filling in the questionnaire. 10 Punkte

Smartphones in school

How could you use your smartphone during lessons? Give two examples.

- ______________________
- ______________________

Would you like to use your phone during breaks? Give two reasons.

☐ Yes ☐ No

- ______________________
- ______________________

Name two problems of using your phone in school and explain them.

- ______________________
- ______________________

Should there be a mobile free zone in school? Say where and why or why not.

____

____

Give two rules for using the smartphone in school safely.

- ______________________
- ______________________

Part 2: Creative writing: The cave

15 Punkte

I was standing in front of the cave's entrance. Around the cave there were several different signs warning people to keep out. I wondered what could be in there. I had a torch, so …

adapted: © BlueRingMedia/Shutterstock

Complete the story.

Include the following aspects:

- what the signs said
- what was in the cave
- what happened next

Write about **60 words**.

Words: ___________

Hauptschulabschlussprüfung Niedersachsen
Englisch 2022

Kurse E und G

I. Listening

Part 1: Questions 1–6

Worksheet
6 Punkte

You will hear six short conversations.
You will hear each conversation twice.
For each question there are three pictures and a short recording.
Choose the correct picture and put a tick (✓) in the box below it.

Example:

0. Which tickets do they buy?

A ☐

B ☐

C ☑

1. What activity would Sally prefer?

A ☐

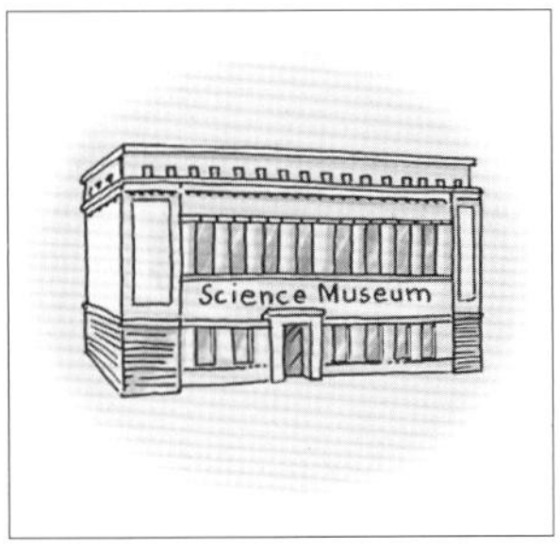

B ☐

C ☐

2. Which extra activity does Paula choose?

A ☐

B ☐

C ☐

3. What does Martha buy?

A ☐

B ☐

C ☐

4. What will Marc do next?

A ☐

B ☐

C ☐

5. What present will Peter buy for Sally's birthday?

A ☐

B ☐

C ☐

6. What pet will the family get?

A ☐

B ☐

C ☐

Kurs E

Part 2: Questions 7–13

A spooky hotel

7 Punkte

Listen to the following interview between Mrs. Moth and Fox Badger from the "z-files Youtube-Channel".
Mrs. Moth talks about a spooky experience in an old hotel in Scotland.
For questions 7–13 tick (✓) the correct box A, B or C.
The first question is an example.

Example:

0. Mrs. Moth gives an interview for …
   - A a magazine. ☐
   - B social media. ☑
   - C a TV show. ☐

7. Mrs. Moth and her husband …
   - A have been to Edinburgh several times. ☐
   - B were in Edinburgh for the first time last year. ☐
   - C went to Edinburgh last month. ☐

8. The hotel was …
   - A in an old castle built 750 years ago. ☐
   - B in an old house built in about 1750. ☐
   - C at 750 Edinburgh Street. ☐

9. When the lights went off Mrs. Moth heard …
   - A someone breathing. ☐
   - B her husband speaking. ☐
   - C the sound from the TV. ☐

10. At first, she thought …
    - A someone was making a joke. ☐
    - B her husband had switched off the light. ☐
    - C the sound was coming from the wardrobe. ☐

11. She saw the ghost …
    - A standing next to her husband. ☐
    - B in the darkness. ☐
    - C after the light came on. ☐

12. The hotel manager told them that …
    - A they were the first people to see the ghost. ☐
    - B other people had seen the ghost before. ☐
    - C the owner of the house first saw the ghost. ☐

13. They …
    - A couldn't sleep in their room. ☐
    - B had to stay in their room. ☐
    - C checked into another room. ☐

Kurs G

Part 2: Questions 7–13

A spooky hotel

7 Punkte

Listen to the following interview between Mrs. Moth and Fox Badger from the "z-files Youtube-Channel".
Mrs. Moth talks about a spooky experience in an old hotel in Scotland.
For questions 7–13 tick (✓) the correct box A, B or C.
The first question is an example.

Example:

0. Mrs. Moth gives an interview for …
   - A a magazine. ☐
   - B social media. ☑
   - C a TV show. ☐

7. Mrs. Moth and her husband …
   - A have been to Edinburgh many times before. ☐
   - B were in Edinburgh for the first time last year. ☐
   - C went to Edinburgh last month. ☐

8. The hotel was …
   - A in a 750-year-old castle. ☐
   - B in an old house from the 1750s. ☐
   - C at 750 Edinburgh Street. ☐

9. In the dark Mrs. Moth heard …
   - A someone breathing. ☐
   - B her husband speaking. ☐
   - C the TV programme. ☐

10. She thought …
    - A someone was making a joke. ☐
    - B her husband had switched off the light. ☐
    - C the sound was coming from the wardrobe. ☐

11. She saw the ghost …
    - A standing next to her husband. ☐
    - B in the darkness. ☐
    - C when the light was on again. ☐

12. The hotel manager said …
    - A they were the first people to see the ghost. ☐
    - B other people had seen the ghost before. ☐
    - C the owner of the house first saw the ghost. ☐

13. They …
    - A couldn't sleep in their room. ☐
    - B had to stay in their room. ☐
    - C moved to another room. ☐

Kurs E

Part 3: Questions 14–21

Monmouth's got Talent

Listen to this announcement for a talent show. It tells you what the talent show is and how you can enter. For questions 14–21, fill in the gaps to complete the notes. The first question is an example.

8 Punkte

0	The popular student event is called	*Monmouth's got Talent.*
14	This year the event is	______________________
15	Britain's got Talent is a BBC	______________________
16	**One** talent the speaker mentions is	______________________
17	This event presents talents from all	______________________
18	Money will be raised for a network of	______________________
19	Send your entry videos to	______________________
20	The winners will be presented on YouTube on	______________________
21	The winner will get	______________________

Kurs G

Part 3: Questions 14–21

Monmouth's got Talent

Listen to this announcement for a talent show. It tells you what the talent show is and how you can enter. For questions 14–21, fill in the gaps to complete the notes. The first question is an example.

8 Punkte

0	The popular student event is called	*Monmouth's got Talent.*
14	This year the event is	______________________
15	Britain's got Talent is a BBC	______________________
16	**One** talent the speaker mentions is	______________________
17	The students taking part are from	______________________

18.	The schools will raise money for a network of	____________ across the UK.
19.	Send your entry videos to	____________ @monmouth.co.uk.
20	You can see the winners on YouTube on	____________
21	The winner will get	____________

Kurs E

Part 4: Questions 22–28

An interview with a musician

7 Punkte

You will hear an interview with Andy Keating, the guitar player of the band IST IST from Manchester. He talks about the effects Covid 19 had on the music industry in greater Manchester.
For questions 22–28 decide whether each sentence is true or false.
Put a tick (✓) in the correct box 'true' or 'false'.
The first question is an example.

		true	false
0.	Andy Keating is the guitar player of the band IST IST.	☑	☐
22.	He is talking about the music business during Covid.	☐	☐
23.	The tickets for the planned concerts were sold out.	☐	☐
24.	Some musicians had to work in other businesses.	☐	☐
25.	Keating says that Covid has not changed the Manchester music scene.	☐	☐
26.	When you want to go to a concert you will have to do a quick Covid test.	☐	☐
27.	The DJ hopes there will soon be cultural events in Manchester again.	☐	☐
28.	IST IST are planning a world tour after the summer.	☐	☐

Kurs G

Part 4: Questions 22–28

An interview with a musician

7 Punkte

You will hear an interview with Andy Keating, the guitar player of the band IST IST from Manchester. He talks about the effects Covid 19 had on the music industry in greater Manchester.
For questions 22–28 decide whether each sentence is true or false.
Put a tick (✓) in the correct box 'true' or 'false'.
The first question is an example.

		true	false
0.	Andy Keating is the guitar player of the band IST IST.	✓	☐
22.	He is talking about the music industry during Covid.	☐	☐
23.	There were no tickets left for the planned concerts.	☐	☐
24.	Some musicians had to work in other jobs.	☐	☐
25.	Keating says the music scene in Manchester is the same after Covid.	☐	☐
26.	When you want to go to a concert you need a quick Covid test.	☐	☐
27.	The DJ hopes that a lot of cultural things will happen in Manchester after Covid.	☐	☐
28.	IST IST are planning a world tour after the summer.	☐	☐

Kurs E

II. Reading

Part 1: Questions 1–6

Read the texts below. Then read the statements (1–6).
Decide whether the statements are **true** or **false**. Then tick (✓) the correct box.

6 Punkte

1.

TEACHING YOU TO BECOME THE PACK LEADER

Fully qualified with 20 years' experience in training Security and Police Protection dogs.

Group training classes on
Wednesday 11 am
Friday 10 am
Saturday 11 am

I offer one-on-one sessions and group training sessions.

HOME BOARDING
Looking after your dogs in my own home if you're going away, where training can be provided if needed with cats, chickens or even other dogs.

Email
dogrehab@gmail.com for more info

First-time clients receive 10 % off!

2.

Bad Art Night: https://www.metrolibrary.org/events/bad-art-night (adapted)

3.

Vegan Baking Class

No dairy, no eggs? No problem!

Our vegan chefs will introduce you to some wonderful vegan ingredients and help you in your quest to master vegan baking.

From nutty chocolate cookies to sticky toffee puddings, we'll inspire your vegan self in this 2-hour online baking session.

This class is fun, relaxed and eggless!

Call us for more information:
01514563219
To take part, register by mail:
info@veganbaking.com

4.

Hamilton Pool Preserve

Hamilton Pool Preserve is a historic swimming hole with a natural 50ft waterfall near Austin/Texas. The waterfall never completely dries up. The preserve is home to a variety of native birds, fish, animals and plants.

Reservations are required to visit. Swimming is not guaranteed.

Additional information:
- Pets are not allowed
- Quarter-mile hike on rough terrain
- Reservations are for up to 8 people and one vehicle

		true	false
1.	You must write an email to sign up for the Bad Art Night.	☐	☐
2.	At the Bad Art Night, you will use old things to create a piece of art.	☐	☐
3.	At Hamilton Pool Preserve you can park next to the waterfall.	☐	☐
4.	For the dog training you can choose between individual or group sessions.	☐	☐
5.	You can take part in the baking class from home.	☐	☐
6.	You can bring your dog to Hamilton Pool Preserve.	☐	☐

Part 2: Questions 7–13

Fancy restaurants

7 Punkte

Read these people's statements about the food they like and the short descriptions of various types of restaurants. Decide which restaurant (**7–13**) is most suitable for which speaker (**A–I**). There are two more speakers than restaurants. Write the correct letter (**A–I**) in the box next to the number. Each letter can only be used once.

A "My girlfriend loves Italian food, especially fresh pasta. I am looking for a romantic spot for a special occasion!" *John, aged 22*

B "I have got quite a short lunch break. Where can I get something decent to eat with good value for money?" *Melissa, aged 27*

C "We like to enjoy dinner, but our kids love to play when they finished their meals. So, we definitely need a place with a playground." *Bob, aged 32*

D "I love eating pizza, pasta and lovely desserts. But because I'm strictly vegan, a restaurant is hard to find." *Chloe, aged 20*

E "My friend has a sweet tooth and I want to take her somewhere special this weekend." *Lucy, aged 16*

F "I really like spicy food. Can you recommend somewhere good in town? I might go to a club afterwards." *Dino, aged 21*

G “At the weekends I like to start with the most important meal of the day. Do you know a place that serves a hearty breakfast and a tasty cappuccino?” *Micky, aged 31*

H “My boyfriend and I love eating fish. But he’s not a big fan of quiet restaurants. He likes entertainment.” *Caroline, aged 19*

I “My girlfriend and I are vegetarian. Can you recommend a suitable restaurant for a healthy lunchtime meal with a delicious sweet treat afterwards?” *Tom, aged 18*

adapted from: https://learnenglishteens.britishcouncil.org/skills/reading/intermediate-b1-reading/food-restaurants

7. ☐ Looking for a restaurant right in the city centre and a perfect location before going on a night out? In this case, *MahaRaja* is the right choice for you. Our specialty is various traditional chicken dishes. But it’s not always the meat that matters. Our veggie food is also really “hot”. For authentic Indian taste there is extra hot.

8. ☐ No matter if you are into elegant dining in a stylish atmosphere for a special evening or if you prefer a delicious lunch in a relaxed setting, *Bella* is the place to go. Our chefs know how to make tasty traditional pasta. Every Friday there is a special Italian night with a great pasta and seafood buffet.

9. ☐ This is the ideal place for people who love sausages, baked beans, bacon and eggs, toast and marmalade for a good start to the day. In *The English Rose Cottage* this is served with a strong cup of breakfast tea, or you can choose from a variety of different coffee specialities. Enjoy your full English brekki at any time during the day and listen to your favourite 1990s songs.

10. ☐ This charming restaurant serves organic food that’s got taste! Come to the *Green Elephant* at lunchtime for our famous super-size burgers with “meat” made from plants. In the afternoon, go for a great fruit salad or enjoy a coffee and a delicious piece of cake. Regionally grown fruit and vegetables.

11. ☐ You haven’t got bags of time but fancy traditional fish and chips or a really tasty hamburger made with the best meat? *Better Quick Bites* is a modern café where food – while served fast – is not junk food! Quality is particularly important here, and our prices are good, too.

12. ☐ *Sweet Treat* is the ideal place for people who are mad about chocolate and sweet snacks. We serve a variety of wonderful desserts, sweets and cakes. Chocolate lovers will be excited by our amazing range of chocolate cakes.

13. ☐ Come inside *Soul Food* and let the good times roll! Our new restaurant has different types of live music every night except Mondays, and excellent food that is cooked with the finest ingredients. There are great fish dishes but also steak and pizza. Join us on Friday nights for the best soul music in town!

Part 3: Questions 14–20

7 Punkte

Read this article about a young woman who didn't use social media for a month. For questions **14–20** tick (✓) the correct box **true** or **false** and **give the line(s) where you find the information**. You will only get a point if both parts of the answer are correct.

3 Things I Learned after a 31 Day Social Media Break

One month ago, I decided I was going to quit social media for one month. So I deleted Snapchat, Instagram, and TikTok.

I spent around 4 hours a day on social media, and when you multiply that by 31 days, I was spending *124 hours a month* on social media. So, I knew that I needed some time off. Now, one month later, I want to describe three of the biggest benefits I received from living life, social media-free.

Improving relationships is probably the most obvious benefit. With my phone, I would check my crush's Snapchat or "stalk" my friends' Instagrams. When I wasn't able to do those things, I instantly felt that my relationships became stronger. Since I could only communicate in-person with people, I found myself valuing the time I spent with them more, and I was even able to find out new things about them.

Learning to love myself was the second benefit. A lot of times, I scrolled through a model or influencer's profile, always comparing my appearance to theirs and trying to be as perfect as they seemed to be. But, without social media, I stopped that and became more confident.

And – last but not least – I stopped being so lazy. One month ago, the first thing I would do after school was sit on the couch and open my phone up to the TikTok "For You" page. Once I got to studying, I still would take long breaks to scroll through my phone. Then, I would have to rush on all my assignments. Today I start my homework as soon as I get home and end up with hours of free time afterwards.

You might have realized now that you have a social media problem, just like I did. So do something about it!

It doesn't have to be as extreme as completely deleting everything: instead, you could set limits on your screen time, or you could make it fun by competing with friends to see who can last the longest without social media. After all, what do you have to lose?

adapted from: https://www.theteenmagazine.com/3-things-i-learned-after-a-31-day-social-media-detox

	true	false	line(s)
0. The author decided to take a social media break.	✓	☐	1
14. The author used to spend more than 120 hours online each month.	☐	☐	______
15. The author wants to show the good sides of a social media break.	☐	☐	______
16. The author says it is difficult to keep up good relationships with friends without social media.	☐	☐	______
17. The author says you may get to know your friends even better without social media.	☐	☐	______

	true	false	line(s)
18. The author thinks it's easier to accept yourself the way you are if you don't look at models or influencers.	☐	☐	______
19. Before her social media break the author used to spend a lot of time on her phone after finishing her homework.	☐	☐	______
20. The author says you must be very strict with yourself to benefit from a social media break.	☐	☐	______

Part 4: Questions 21–27

7 Punkte

Read the following article about a funny event in Poland.
Match the first parts of the sentences (**21–27**) with the sentence endings (**A–I**).
There are more sentence endings than you need.

Croissant scare

A lot of people are afraid of spiders, but have you ever heard of people being afraid of croissants?

Believe it or not, one of these traditional French sweet breakfast rolls scared many residents of the Polish city of Krakow. Elzbieta Wojcik, aged 76, looked out of her kitchen window last March and saw a strange brown object hanging in a tree. She thought it was a kind of dangerous animal and warned her neighbours. The residents were so worried that they kept their windows closed for a couple of days. In the end they called for help to get the "animal" removed from the tree opposite their apartment building.

Later, the Krakow Animal Welfare Society wrote on its Facebook account that a woman called the authorities to report an unidentified animal sitting in the tree. Animal welfare officers phoned the residents in the building and asked them to describe the animal. One resident explained that the animal looked like a large brown bird; another said it was a kind of lizard.

Although the inspectors knew that it was almost impossible that a reptile would survive the cool spring temperatures in the southern Polish city, they wondered if the animal could have been an unwanted pet thrown out by its owners.

The animal welfare officer explained what happened: He said he went to the apartment building where the residents lived to check on the strange animal. He reported that he spotted a "brown creature sitting on a tree branch," and that its "brown fur was shining in the sun". He then added: "The poor little thing had no legs or head." When he discovered that the strange beast was a croissant, probably thrown out of a window to feed the birds, he was "almost swept off his feet by a laughing attack". "But", he said "Better safe than sorry!" The public should continue to be careful and report any sightings of strange animals.

adapted from: https://breakingnewsenglish.com/2104/210418-croissant.html

		A	didn't open their windows for some days.
21.	People in Krakow were afraid	B	an unidentified animal.
22.	They were so afraid that they	C	would survive in cold weather.
23.	The woman told the authorities about	D	started laughing.
24.	One person described the thing as	E	of a croissant hanging in a tree.
25.	The officer first thought it	F	report unusual things.
26.	When the officer found out what the thing was, he	G	could be an unwanted pet.
27.	The authorities want people to	H	of feeding birds.
		I	a large brown bird.

21.	22.	23.	24.	25.	26.	27.

III. Writing: Set I

Part 1: AppWhats photo message: At the airport

You are at the airport waiting for your flight and you send this picture to your friend Kevin. He wants to know more about your holiday plans.

10 Punkte

Guess where I am.
I am so excited!

Kevin: Oh wow, you are at the airport! Where are you going?

You: ______________________________

____

Kevin: Oh, I didn't know. **When** did you decide that and **why** are you going there?

You: ______________________________

____

Kevin: Who's with you?

You: ______________________________

____

Kevin: What do you plan to do there? **Which** places do you want to see?

You: ______________________________

____

Kevin: Where are you staying?

You: ______________________________

____

Kevin: How long will you stay? **When** will you be back?

You: ______________________________

____

Kevin: Wow, I would love to see more pictures. Do you think we can meet after your trip?

You: ______________________________

____

Bild: Dima Moro/shutterstock

Part 2: Writing an article – One day without electricity

15 Punkte

Last Thursday there was no electricity and no internet in your village. Write an article for your school magazine about your day without electricity.

- What was your first reaction?
- What was difficult?
- Which things didn't work and what did you use instead?
- How did you spend your day?

https://kurzelinks.de/y5p1

Write about **80 words**.

Words: ___________

III. Writing: Set II

Part 1: Application form for a talent show

You want to take part in a talent show. Before they invite you, you have to fill in this application form.

10 Punkte

Application Form "Talent Show"

Name: ______________________ Date of birth: ______________________

Gender: ______________________ Email: ______________________

Describe your talent in detail. ______________________

____

What equipment do you need for your performance? ______________________

____

Tell us something about yourself. (hobbies, family …) ______________________

____

What would you do if you won the 500 Euro prize? ______________________

____

How long did it take you to practise your performance? ______________________

____

How did you find out about the contest? ______________________

____

Which two people would you like to invite? ______________________

____

Part 2: A short story: A box on the doorstep

15 Punkte

Read the beginning of the story and finish it.

Last night when he came home, he found a box on his doorstep. He hadn't ordered anything …

Image Source/iStock

Write about **80 words**.
Include the following ideas:

- What was in the box?
- Who was it from?
- How did he feel?
- What happened next?

Words: ______

Kurs G

II. Reading

Part 1: Questions 1–6

Read the texts below. Then read the statements (1–6).
Decide whether the statements are **true** or **false**. Then tick (✓) the correct box.

7 Punkte

1.

TEACHING YOU TO BECOME THE PACK LEADER

Fully qualified with 20 years' experience in training Security and Police Protection dogs.

Group training classes on
Wednesday 11 am
Friday 10 am
Saturday 11 am

I offer one-on-one sessions and group training sessions.

Email
dogrehab@gmail.com for more info

First-time clients receive 10 % off!

2.

3.

Vegan Baking Class

No dairy, no eggs? No problem!

Our vegan chefs will introduce you to some wonderful vegan ingredients and help you in your quest to master vegan baking.

From nutty chocolate cookies to sticky toffee puddings, we'll inspire your vegan self in this 2-hour online baking session.

This class is fun, relaxed and eggless!

4.

Hamilton Pool Preserve

Hamilton Pool Preserve is a historic swimming hole with a natural 50ft waterfall near Austin/Texas. The waterfall never completely dries up.

Reservations are required to visit. Swimming is not guaranteed.

Additional information:
- Pets are not allowed
- Quarter-mile hike on rough terrain
- Reservations are for up to 8 people and one vehicle

Bad Art Night: https://www.metrolibrary.org/events/bad-art-night (adapted)

		true	false
1.	You must write an email to sign up for the Bad Art Night.	☐	☐
2.	At the Bad Art Night, you will use old things to create a piece of art.	☐	☐
3.	At Hamilton Pool Preserve you can park next to the waterfall.	☐	☐
4.	For the dog training you can choose between individual or group sessions.	☐	☐

	true	false
5. You can take part in the baking class from home.	☐	☐
6. You can bring your dog to Hamilton Pool Preserve.	☐	☐

Part 2: Questions 7–13

Fancy restaurants

7 Punkte

Read these people's statements about the food they like and the short descriptions of various types of restaurants. Decide which restaurant (**7–13**) is most suitable for which speaker (**A–H**). There is one more speaker than restaurants. Write the correct letter (**A–H**) in the box next to the number. Each letter can only be used once.

A	"My girlfriend loves Italian food, especially fresh pasta. I am looking for a romantic spot for a special occasion!" *John, aged 22*
B	"I have got quite a short lunch break. Where can I get something to eat with good value for money?" *Melissa, aged 27*
C	"I love eating pizza, pasta and lovely desserts. But because I'm strictly vegan, a restaurant is hard to find." *Chloe, aged 20*
D	"My friend likes everything sweet and I want to take her somewhere special this weekend." *Lucy, aged 16*
E	"I really like spicy food. Can you recommend somewhere good in town? I might go to a club afterwards." *Dino, aged 21*
F	"At the weekends I like to start with the most important meal of the day. Do you know a place that serves a great breakfast and a tasty cappuccino?" *Micky, aged 31*
G	"My boyfriend and I love eating fish. But he's not a big fan of quiet restaurants. He likes entertainment." *Caroline, aged 19*
H	"My girlfriend and I are vegetarian. Can you recommend a restaurant for a healthy lunchtime meal with a delicious sweet treat afterwards?" *Tom, aged 18*

adapted from: https://learnenglishteens.britishcouncil.org/skills/reading/intermediate-b1-reading/food-restaurants

7. ☐ Looking for a restaurant right in the city centre and a perfect location before going on a night out? In this case, *MahaRaja* is the right choice for you. Our speciality is traditional chicken dishes. But it's not always the meat that matters. Our veggie food is also really "hot".

8. ☐ If you like elegant dining in a stylish atmosphere for a special evening or if you prefer a delicious and relaxed lunch, *Bella* is the place to go. Our chefs know how to make tasty traditional pasta.

9. ☐ *The English Rose Cottage* is the ideal place for people who love sausages, baked beans, bacon and eggs, toast and marmalade for a good start to the day. There you can choose between a strong cup of breakfast tea and a variety of different coffee specialities. Enjoy your full English brekki at any time during the day and listen to your favourite 1990s songs.

10. ☐ This charming restaurant serves organic food that's got taste! Come to the *Green Elephant* at lunchtime for our famous super-size burgers with "meat" made from plants. In the afternoon, go for a great fruit salad or enjoy a coffee and a delicious piece of cake. Regionally grown fruit and vegetables.

11. ☐ You haven't got a lot of time but like traditional fish and chips or a really tasty hamburger made with the best meat? *Better Quick Bites* is a modern café where food – while served fast – is not junk food! Quality is important here, and our prices are good, too.

12. ☐ *Sweet Treat* is the ideal place for people who are mad about chocolate and sweet snacks. We serve a variety of desserts, sweets and cakes. Chocolate lovers will be excited by our amazing chocolate cakes.

13. ☐ Come inside *Soul Food* and let the good times roll! Our new restaurant has different types of live music every night except Mondays, and our chef cooks excellent food with the finest ingredients. There are great fish dishes but also steak and pizza. Join us on Friday nights for the best soul music in town!

Adapted from: https://learnenglishteens.britishcouncil.org/skills/reading/intermediate-b1-reading/food-restaurants

Part 3: Questions 14–20

Read this article about a young woman who didn't use social media for a month. For questions **14–20** tick (✓) the correct box **true** or **false** and **give the line(s) where you find the information**. You will only get a point if both parts of the answer are correct.

7 Punkte

3 Things I Learned after a 31 Day Social Media Break

One month ago, I stopped using social media and deleted Snapchat, Instagram, and TikTok.

Before that I spent around 4 hours a day on social media. That means 124 hours a month.

So, I knew that I needed some time off. Now, one month later, I want to tell you about the three biggest benefits I got from living social media-free.

Better relationships are probably the greatest benefit. With my phone, I always checked my crush's Snapchat or "stalked" my friends' Instagrams. When I wasn't able to do those things, I felt that my relationships became stronger. The time I spent with my friends was more special because I could only communicate with them face-to-face. I was even able to find out new things about them.

Learning to love myself was another benefit. A lot of times, I scrolled through a model or influencer's profile. I always compared my appearance to theirs and tried to be as perfect as they seemed to be. But, without social media, I stopped comparing and became more confident.

And – last but not least – I stopped being so lazy. One month ago, the first thing I did after school was sit on the couch and open TikTok on my phone. Once I started studying, I still took long breaks to scroll through my phone. Then, I had to rush on all my homework.

Today I do my homework as soon as I get home and have hours of free time afterwards.
Maybe you have realized now that you have a social media problem, just like I did. So do something about it!
It doesn't have to be as extreme as completely deleting everything: instead, you could set limits on your screen time. After all, what do you have to lose?
adapted from: https://www.theteenmagazine.com/3-things-i-learned-after-a-31-day-social-media-detox

	true	false	line(s)
0. The author decided to take a social media break.	☑	☐	1
14. The author spent more than 120 hours online each month.	☐	☐	______
15. The author wants to show the good sides of a social media break.	☐	☐	______
16. The author says it is difficult to keep up good relationships with friends without social media.	☐	☐	______
17. The author says you may get to know your friends better without social media.	☐	☐	______
18. The author thinks it's easier to accept yourself the way you are if you don't look at models or influencers.	☐	☐	______
19. Before her social media break, the author always spent a lot of time on her phone after finishing her homework.	☐	☐	______
20. The author says you must be very strict with yourself to see the positive effects of a social media break.	☐	☐	______

Part 4: Questions 21–27

7 Punkte

Read the following article about a funny event in Poland. Match the first parts of the sentences (**21–27**) with the sentence endings (**A–H**). There are more sentence ending than you need.

Croissant Scare

A lot of people are afraid of spiders, but have you ever heard of people being afraid of croissants?
Believe it or not, one of these traditional French sweet breakfast rolls scared some people in Krakow, Poland. Elzbieta Wojcik, aged 76, looked out of her kitchen window last March and saw a strange brown object hanging in a tree. She thought it was a kind of dangerous animal and warned her neighbours. They were so worried that they kept their windows closed for a couple of days. In the end they called for help to get the "animal" removed from the tree.
Later, the Krakow Animal Welfare Society reported that a woman called the police because there was an unidentified animal sitting in the tree. Animal welfare officers

asked the people living in the building to describe the animal. One explained that the animal looked like a large brown bird; another said it was a kind of lizard. The inspectors thought it couldn't be a reptile because it wouldn't survive the cool spring temperatures. They wondered if the animal could have been an unwanted pet thrown out by its owners.
The animal welfare officer said he went to the apartment building to check on the strange animal. He later reported that he saw a "brown creature sitting on a tree branch," and that its "brown fur was shining in the sun". He then added: "The poor little thing had no legs or head." When he found out that it was only a croissant, he was "almost swept off his feet by a laughing attack".
"But", he said "Better safe than sorry!" The public should continue to be careful and report any sightings of strange animals to the police.

adapted from: https://breakingnewsenglish.com/2104/210418-croissant.html

		A	didn't open their windows for some days.
21.	People in Krakow were afraid	B	an unidentified animal.
22.	They were so afraid that they	C	would survive in cold weather.
23.	The woman told the police about	D	started laughing.
24.	One person described the thing as	E	of a croissant hanging in a tree.
25.	The officer first thought it	F	report unusual things.
26.	When the officer found out what the thing was, he	G	could be an unwanted pet.
27.	The police want people to	H	a large brown bird.

21.	22.	23.	24.	25.	26.	27.

III. Writing: Set I

Part 1: AppWhats photo message: At the airport

10 Punkte

You are at the airport waiting for your flight and you send this picture to your friend Kevin. He wants to know more about your holiday plans.

Guess where I am.
I am so excited!

Kevin: Oh wow, you are at the airport! Where are you going?

You: ______________________________

Kevin: Oh, I didn't know. **When** did you decide that and **why** are you going there?

You: ______________________________

Kevin: Who's with you?

You: ______________________________

Kevin: **What** do you plan to do there? **Which** places do you want to see?

You: ______________________________

Kevin: Where are you staying?

You: ______________________________

Kevin: How long will you stay? **When** will you be back?

You: ______________________________

Kevin: Wow, I would love to see more pictures. Do you think we can meet after your trip?

You: ______________________________

Bild: Dima Moro/shutterstock

Part 2: Writing an article – One day without electricity

15 Punkte

Last Thursday there was no electricity and no internet in your village.
Write an article for your school magazine about your day without electricity.

- What was your first reaction?
- What was difficult?
- Which things didn't work and what did you use instead?
- How did you spend your day?

https://kurzelinks.de/y5p1

Write about **60 words**.

Words: ___________

III. Writing: Set II

Part 1: Application form for a talent show

You want to take part in a talent show. Before they invite you, you have to fill in this application form.

Application Form "Talent Show"

Name: ______________ Date of birth: ______________

Gender: ______________ Email: ______________

Describe your talent in detail. ______________

____

What equipment do you need for your performance? ______________

____

Tell us something about yourself. (hobbies, family …) ______________

____

What would you do if you won the 500 Euro prize? ______________

____

How long did it take you to practise your performance? ______________

____

How did you find out about the contest? ______________

____

Which two people would you like to invite? ______________

____

Part 2: A short story: A box on the doorstep

15 Punkte

Read the beginning of the story and finish it.

Last night when he came home, he found a box on his doorstep. He hadn't ordered anything …

Write about **60 words**. Include the following ideas:

- What was in the box?
- Who was it from?
- How did he feel?
- What happened next?

Image Source/iStock

Words: ___________

Hauptschulabschlussprüfung Niedersachsen
Englisch 2023

Um dir die Prüfung 2023 schnellstmöglich zur Verfügung stellen zu können, bringen wir sie in digitaler Form heraus.

Sobald die Original-Prüfungsaufgaben 2023 freigegeben sind, können sie als PDF auf der Online-Plattform *MyStark* heruntergeladen werden. Deinen persönlichen Zugangscode findest du auf der Umschlaginnenseite vorne im Buch.

Aktuelle Prüfung

www.stark-verlag.de/mystark